KU-001-400

Peirene

HANNE ØRSTAVIK

TRANSLATED FROM THE
NORWEGIAN BY DEBORAH DAWKIN

Like sant som jeg er virkelig

AUTHOR

With the publication of her first novel in 1994, Hanne Ørstavik, born in 1969, embarked on a career that has made her one of the most admired authors in contemporary Norwegian literature. Her literary breakthrough came three years later with the publication of *Love* (*Kjærlighet*), which in 2006 was voted the sixth best Norwegian book of the last twenty-five years. Since then the author has written several acclaimed novels and has received a number of literary prizes, including the Dobloug Prize, for her entire literary output, and the Brage Prize, Norway's most prestigious literary award. Ørstavik's novels have been translated into eighteen languages but never, until now, into English.

TRANSLATOR

Deborah Dawkin trained as an actress, and worked in theatre for ten years. She has written creatively and dramatized works, including the poetry of the Norwegian Inger Hagerup. Other translations include *Ugly Bugly* and *Fatso*, both by Lars Ramslie, and *To Music* by Ketil Bjørnstad, which was nominated for the Independent Foreign Fiction Prize.

MEIKE ZIERVOGEL
PEIRENE PRESS

Everyone who has read
Fifty Shades of Grey should
read this book. Why?
The Blue Room holds up
a mirror to a part of the
female psyche that yearns for
submission. The story shows
how erotic fantasies are
formed by the relationship
with our parents. It then
delves further to analyse
the struggle of women
to separate from their
mothers – a struggle that is
rarely addressed in either
literature or society.

First published in Great Britain in 2014 by
Peirene Press Ltd
17 Cheverton Road
London N19 3BB
www.peirenepress.com

First published under the original Norwegian language title
Like sant som jeg er virkelig
Copyright © 1999, Forlaget Oktober A/S, Oslo

This translation © Deborah Dawkin, 2014

Hanne Ørstavik asserts her moral right to be identified as the author of
this work in accordance with the Copyright, Designs and Patents Act, 1988.

All rights reserved. No part of this publication may be reproduced or
transmitted in any form or by any means, electronic or mechanical,
including photocopy, recording, or any information storage and
retrieval system, without permission in writing from the publisher.

This book is sold subject to the condition that it shall
not be resold, lent, hired out or otherwise circulated
without the express prior consent of the publisher.

ISBN 978-1-908670-15-1

This book is a work of fiction. Names, characters, businesses,
organizations, places and events are either the product of the
author's imagination or used fictitiously. Any resemblance to actual
persons, living or dead, events or locales is entirely coincidental.

Designed by Sacha Davison Lunt
Photographic image by Rekha Garton / Flickr Open / Getty Images
Typeset by Tetragon, London
Printed and bound by T J International, Padstow, Cornwall

This project has been published with the financial support of NORLA.

This project has been funded with support from
the European Commission. This publication reflects
the views only of the author, and the Commission
cannot be held responsible for any use which may
be made of the information contained therein.

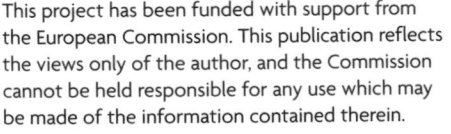

HANNE ØRSTAVIK

TRANSLATED FROM THE NORWEGIAN
BY DEBORAH DAWKIN

Peirene

The
Blue Room

I cannot get out. Something must have happened to the lock. I'll have to wait until Mum comes home from work to help me. Everything was totally normal when I went to bed last night. It was late and I dropped straight off to sleep. This morning I was woken up by the sound of the front door. I looked at the clock. It was quarter past six. I assumed Mum had got up early and had just gone to fetch the paper, but then I heard nothing more.

I'm standing by the window, looking up at the sky. It's so quiet here in my room, it feels padded, like a cocoon. My armpits are damp; occasionally a drop of moisture trickles down. My hands are cold and dry. The sky is clear, but it's windy, and now a dark cloud is approaching. A moment ago a plane came into view, like a tiny dart, its exhaust as straight as an arrow. I stood here and watched it disappear.

I lay in for a while, smiling to myself under the warmth of the duvet. But I knew I wouldn't go back to sleep. I was too excited. I was looking forward to my coffee and to all that was going to happen. I climbed down from my loft bed and went over to the door. But it was shut. It took some time before I realized I wouldn't get it open. I pulled at the handle, as hard as I could without it coming off, since it's old and broken. And then it struck me: I was never going to get out on my own, someone was going to have to help me. I started shouting. I banged on the wall of the lounge, where Mum sleeps, and then on the kitchen wall. We share the third wall with the next-door apartment. I've no idea who lives there. The wall is thick and I've never heard a sound from behind it. I didn't try that one. The fourth has a window in it, but I'm naked. I'd put the clothes I wore yesterday into the washing machine in the bathroom and my wardrobe is out in the hall. I wrapped a sheet round me, but then I stopped myself: it seems daft to go screaming from the fourth floor into a backyard in Frogner. I've sent up a prayer that everything will be all right. I've decided to leave it to God, to put my fate in his hands. White empty spaces interrupt my thoughts when I try to think logically and then I can't remember what I was thinking. I must try to breathe from my stomach, try to relax and not tense my muscles. I suddenly remember some exercises from an evening class in bioenergetic training. Only postgraduate students were supposed to attend the class really, but I managed to sneak in. I take my duvet, spread it on the floor and lie on my back. Just imagine if I hadn't studied psychology and didn't have an insight into extreme reactions. I try to push the air up and down in my stomach. I close my eyes so I don't have to see my body. The trick is to relax so much that the small of your back touches the floor, but I find that very difficult. I'm useless at concentrating on physical things. My brain finds it dull and then my thoughts start wandering. It's nearly eight o'clock now. I see Ivar standing next to the open window of his apartment, smoking a cigarette in the fresh morning air. He's wearing his red and black Icelandic sweater, the one that's frayed at the wrists. I think about his hands, his mouth round his cigarette, his lips. And then he smiles, a calm, warm, happy smile that touches my whole being. He'll be leaving soon. He'll walk down the stairs and out through the gates, turn right into the street. It will be fine, I think to myself, I will get out of here in time. And yet, it's as if I already know it's over. I must let it go, let go of the hope and the dreams, let them float away like twigs in a stream. Rucksack, guitar case, his feet as he steps onto the Airport Express. He was supposed to turn as he got onto the train, and I was supposed to be standing there, on the platform, carrying my case, out of breath and happy. I was supposed to arrive just in time. I still can. If only I get out now. Then I'll run with my bag down to the station. And there I'll be. He'll look at me with that same expression in his eyes as he had on that first day: Hi there! At the back entrance of the Social Sciences block, where the bikes are kept. I remember how he startled me, how I stopped in my tracks. He was just the new boy working in the canteen back then. He looked at me, and it felt as though he'd poked me in the stomach with a sharp stick. He was wearing faded jeans and a short white jacket; he held his left arm tightly across his chest and tucked under his right armpit as he smoked, one knee bent, a foot wedged up against the red-brick wall. His voice was deeper than I'd expected. Not that I'd ever thought about his voice before. Or had I? I'd seen him behind the counter, but he was rarely serving at the tills; he did other things – buttered baguettes, chopped tomatoes – standing in the background. It all seems so long ago now. Come with me, he said, and you can borrow a towel. He dropped his cigarette butt into the red bucket, exhaled from the corner of his mouth and held the door open for me. He smiled again and walked towards the canteen, leaving me standing in the entrance hall next to the information desk. I watched him disappear through the swing doors where they take the dirty dishes on trolleys. My glasses were covered with rain. I took them off, thinking I should find some tissue to dry them with. My clothes were drenched. I was sweating, and my skirt was dripping and clinging to my legs. Everything had gone wrong. I'd had to stay at home and study because Mum couldn't get the time off work, so I had to be there to let the plumber in. And then he'd turned up late so I lost a lot of time. I'd cycled here as fast as I could, but when I finally arrived and wanted to lock up my bike, I realized I'd lost the chain. I knew I'd put it under the clip – I always keep it clamped on the rear rack, I do it automatically. It must have fallen off. There had been a light drizzle as I set off from home; by the time I arrived it was pelting down. In just three minutes the lecture would start. I couldn't leave my bike without locking it: I couldn't afford to lose it, and I wouldn't be able to concentrate on the lecture if I was worrying about my bike being stolen. Everything was going wrong. But I had to cycle back and look. As I pedalled down Blindernveien and past Marienlyst School I started to cry. The lock was lying next to the Portakabins outside the Norwegian Broadcasting Corporation building, a blue-plastic-covered chain. I got off and picked it up, hung it over the handlebar, turned and pushed my bike all the way back — uphill — crying the whole way. I had to lock it in a different place from usual. As I stood there in the entrance hall, I was still crying – or the tears were flowing at least. It must be physiological, I thought, as if I had a plastic bag in my chest filled with water. But my face was so wet with rain, I don't think he noticed the tears. I felt a stabbing pain in my left eyebrow. I was going to be late for my lecture. At the same time, I wanted to follow the canteen man, to be wherever he was. Yes, that was what I wanted. That was the truth. Already then. I walked towards the glass partition that marks the start of the canteen. Perhaps I should go and look for him, tell him I had to go. Or perhaps he'd forgotten me, since it was taking so long. Then again, he might be standing in there laughing at me. He reappeared through the swing doors and walked calmly towards me, holding a clean white kitchen towel, neatly folded, in his outstretched hand. Here, he said. I smiled and thanked him, and he asked if I wanted a coffee. I ought to go to my lecture. There'd still be quarter of an hour left. I glanced at my watch. Yes, at least that. I looked at him. My whole forehead was throbbing. Come back with the towel later then. Yes, I said, thanks. He smiled, broadly, as though amused by something. He seemed almost too happy, I wasn't sure I could quite trust his smile. I went down the wide spiral staircase to the toilets, taking three steps at a time. Luckily nobody was there. I stood in front of the big mirror and had to smile. I could see why he'd laughed. My red hair was sticking out in a clump on either side of my face, my gold hairclip had slipped at an angle, making my hair bulge on top, and my mascara had left dark tracks under my eyes. I wiped my face with the towel energetically, blew my nose, dried my eyes – I had finally stopped crying – polished my glasses, ran back up the stairs and hurried to Auditorium 7. I opened the door carefully, sat at the very back and took a notepad out of my bag. The top corners were damp. I looked down on the lecturer. He seemed so small, whizzing about, drawing jagged lines on the board next to the overhead projector. There was something aggressive about him: no doubt he was irritated by people coming in late, causing a disturbance – he was in the middle of explaining cognitive dissonance and attribution theory.

I stayed in the auditorium during the break to copy my neighbour's notes. Kind of her to let me; more than 500 of us will compete for thirty-seven places, so she didn't have to, but she offered. You can see the competitiveness among some of the boys. The resolute gaze, the arm covering their notes. As I wrote, it all started to make sense, travelling through my hand and into my body, and the calm concentration, the logical lines, put me in a state of suspension. And yet that face. Taking form and then evaporating. Taking form and disappearing. Like a pulse – the canteen man, his smile, his eyes – an image lodged in my bloodstream so that each time it pumped past my eyes, it became visible again. I smiled. Stop it, Johanne. I shook my head to make it go away. I'd moved down to the third row, where I usually sit, in front of the lecturer. I couldn't stop smiling. It was almost a need. Although I'm not sure I knew where this smile was coming from yet. After the break the auditorium began to fill up again, footsteps and voices in the air like dust settling all around. Resuming its place, like sunshine and warmth after a storm. The lecture could begin once more, like a symphony. I must have felt finely tuned, infinitely joyous and light. I remember humming a song in my head: Every day thy riches grow, For Jesus Christ has made it so, Though doubt and sin thy life may fill, A place in heaven awaits thee still.

I get up and go back to the window, the sheet covering me. The sky is so light and open. My exercises haven't had the least effect. I don't understand people who swear by body therapies, who seem happy to stretch and pummel and rub, believing these activities offer a path to inner understanding. Ultimately it is through thought that we discriminate or make decisions. The physical may act as a signpost, but the mind does the work and passes judgement. I run my fingers along the window ledge; the paintwork is flaking. I've told Mum that we ought to keep it in good repair, scrape and paint it, but nothing has happened so far. There are bubbles, tiny blisters, here and there. How do we recognize when something starts? I think of the beginnings of various things in my life: my studies, my desire to be a psychologist, this thing with Ivar, my connection with God. Only in retrospect does a starting point become clear, something I can pin down to a particular book read at a certain moment, the light on those trees on that day, glimpsing a brown dog at a particular spot, the sound of the church bells ringing. But the fact is, there are no true beginnings, everything

connects. And this continual interconnectedness consti-
tutes original sin. But what do we do with the guilt? Being
ignorant of the moment things begin, we can repeatedly
deny guilt, pointing ever further back to a previous event
as the starting point – it wasn't me. I prefer to think the
opposite. To think of myself as guilty of everything, thus
giving me a responsibility and a duty to change. Everything
should be as new. The train is about to leave. I'll never
make it. Ivar is sitting by the window now, looking out,
going through the old town, up over Groruddalen, past
the Salvation Army by Alna Bridge, gazing out over the
dark stream before Bryn, the workmen's barracks, the
industrial park, the motorways, the Cooperative Dairy,
people waiting on station platforms going to town. Gestalt
psychology began in 1913 with intermittent flashes of light
seen through the window of a train by a young Jewish
woman in Germany. She noticed that if these repeated
bursts of light came at short enough intervals, her eye was
unable to distinguish them and she perceived them as one
unbroken streak. A single streak of light. She got out at
the first station, her mind in turmoil, knowing that she
was badly needed in Vienna, where she'd been heading,
to look after a recently widowed aunt who could barely
walk due to the pain of a pelvic prolapse. Where does pain
go? Has anyone researched pain? Might it be a form of
energy? Can it be recycled? Can we reuse it? I remember
scribbling these thoughts in the margin. I looked up,
turned in my chair; my skirt was still pretty damp, but
my hair was almost dry. I looked at all the students sitting

around me reading. I remember being filled with a sense of love for them. I had so much to give. I was pleased with my thoughts about pain. I wanted some canteen coffee, imagined a white paper cup filled with dark-brown, steaming liquid. I wanted to go down to the canteen and buy one. But I had to be firm with myself. Remember the money, Johanne, I said, it's a waste when you've got a full Thermos, and think of the time too. Focus, Johanne. Concentrate. Anyway, the young woman got off the train and vanished. She found a room near a university where she and three other young Jewish women – all of whom eventually went to America – developed a theory about the isomorphic functioning of the brain. The human brain recognizes identical patterns. And when the senses only pick up fragments, our brain fills in the gaps to achieve wholeness and harmony. Thus flashes of light become a streak when viewed at certain intervals, just as we tend to see a whole circle when presented with a ring with a break in it. There is, in fact, only an arc, but the brain says 'circle'. Whenever I see a white jacket my brain says 'canteen man'. I got up after all. I took a ten-kroner piece from my pencil case, picked up the wet towel from the floor, walked out of the reading room and went down the stairs to the canteen. I felt light, weightless, as though my body didn't exist.

The noise in the canteen was like a fog, a cacophony that closed in around me like a membrane, soft and fine. I was here for a purpose, of course, I had to return the towel. I walked up to the counter, but couldn't see him anywhere. I considered going to the swing doors by the dirty dishes and peeping in. A tall trolley was pushed aside and I caught sight of him, chopping at a bench, his back turned to me, hand on knife, neck bent, a thigh, everything utterly silent, in slow motion, like a movie. Somebody shouted at him. He turned and looked along the line of people at the counter, as though registering the queue, its length, then his gaze returned, flitting a little before it finally fixed on me. We looked at each other. He put down his knife and walked towards me. He said something to a girl arranging cheese rolls on a tray; she was pretty, yet he looked only at me, nodded towards the swing doors, smiling all the while. You are here in my belly, I thought, living inside me already, or perhaps that's a recent idea, but I felt it even then, I had to scold my legs to make them move. Walk, I said. My body felt so hot, I think I was filled with laughter.

We must forgive seven times seventy times, and he who looks back will be turned into a pillar of salt. I lie on the bed, my loft bed, staring out of the window. It is so light. Is it always so bright in here at this time? I can't remember being in bed so late in the morning before. But the apartment is quite high and there is almost nothing but sky outside. Mum called it the Tower when we first moved here. Like on a castle. Poor Mum, she deserves some peace, and to relax. I close my eyes. There's an Asian girl chained to the bed. Twelve years old. It is an iron bed with rails and there are bars at the window. A fat sweaty man comes once an hour. He takes off his shorts and shirt, and she has to do whatever he wants. Perhaps he orders her to suck him. The little-girl-mouth stretches tightly around his big cock. I see her little hole in front of me. She is thin, her skin smooth and golden. He wants her to sit on him. She does what he says, doesn't talk, doesn't smile. Just does. Does and does. And then comes the sperm. Then maybe he cries. It takes only fifteen minutes, or seven, or three. He straddles the basin and washes himself with water from a jug, then dresses and leaves, and she has a chain around her ankle. It's attached to the bed and she can go only as far as the window. She looks out. Down into the street, where she sees the man walking along, talking to another girl who works there. A grey sun in a white sky. Or maybe she lies on the bed trying not to hear the sounds from the other rooms. Perhaps she wonders what she'll get for dinner today. I try to imagine what it's like to be there. I think how awful it must be not to know who's coming. Whether he'll be cruel or kind. I think about what the bad ones might do, beat her perhaps, or stick bottles up her arse. I clamber down from my bed. My back feels better, soft and supple. Perhaps nothing's actually happened. It's only quarter past nine. I'll take a quick shower and call a cab. Perhaps the door was just jammed, a bit of bad luck. Imagine if this whole thing is in my head and I've simply not managed to open the door until now.

I go down on my knees and peer through the keyhole. I can see a section of the kitchen: the cooker and the fridge, a corner of the table, and Mum's chair. I picture her as she sat there, rigid, as though somebody had poured aspic over her, sticky layers of gelatine. She put her hands together to sing grace. I joined in. She sang loudly, out of tune, she seemed oblivious to it. We smiled at each other and began to eat. I felt like Ivar was there, standing beside the table all through the meal, watching me. I told Mum about the plumber, about my bicycle lock and the rain, that a boy who worked in the canteen had lent me a towel, and that he was called Ivar. A thoughtful gesture, don't you think? I looked over at her. She appeared to be engrossed in her food. He was so kind, I said. I tried to speak in my normal voice. Ivar. Just talking about him made me smile. I didn't want Mum to notice. We were having pie, my favourite. I'd cooked it because I felt happy, as though I had something to celebrate. What is he studying? asked Mum. Her expression was serious, brow furrowed, voice sharp. I'm not sure, I said, whether he's studying anything, we hardly talked, I just took the towel back to him, and then someone dropped a tray of lasagne and he had to go in and help. Mum looked out of the window, head turned, gazing up at the sky. We could do with some sunshine, Johanne, an Indian summer, that's what we need, don't you think? I couldn't tell her the rest, the details. Or that we had in fact talked a bit. Every detail of what he'd said echoed in my head: his name, the way he'd said it, his country dialect, soft and unassuming, a voice that seemed to open up onto wide horizons. When I'd suggested he must find it frustrating to work shut up in a kitchen, he'd said he conjured up images of the Hardanger Plateau, and he walked miles every day, he said, but pretended he had heather underfoot, and it was good training for the hunt. I'd nodded in agreement, but when he smiled at me, I realized he'd been joking. He lived near Gamle Aker. He could see the church from his window. Surely a sign, I thought. I didn't tell him that I was a Christian. I was frightened he wouldn't like it. Forgive me, Father, for my frailty. Mum said she had a visitor coming. She looked out of the window as she talked. I felt I'd betrayed her by not sharing my thoughts. I should tell her, keep her informed. My left eyebrow twitched, I had to rub it with my finger. Mum turned towards me; she looked sad. I wanted to comfort her. She probably knew I was keeping something from her. I wanted to make her happy. I'm going to Friday Mass, I said, I'll have to go soon. Johanne, she said, inclining her head, have you done something to your hair? No, I said, touching it; from the way she was talking it sounded as if it had caught fire. You've sort of lost your curls, said Mum. No, I said, it's my hairclip pinning them back. I'm so awfully tired, said Mum, turning to the window again. She had finished her pie, but there was a lot of salad on her plate still. You should eat your greens, Mum, I said. You're so strict, she said, taking her packet of cigarettes out. I leant my chair back to shut the door to my room and stop the smoke going in. She lit up and we stared out of the window onto the backyard. From my chair I can see the big birch tree. The leaves were red and yellow. We'd had a few nights of frost. From Mum's chair you can see the Virginia creeper on the grey wall to the side of the courtyard. It too had already begun to turn red. Suddenly her plate fell to the floor, sending iceberg lettuce, pieces of tomato, sweetcorn everywhere. I turned to her. She looked so small as she sat gazing out of the window. I don't think she'd even noticed the plate, or heard it fall. She's been through so much. I crouched down and began to pick up the bits. They should be nicer to her at work, I thought, so she has some energy left when she comes home. I don't know much about Mum's work really. She works in the Culture Department. She trained as a teacher originally, but she has higher qualifications in art education; her work generally seems to involve schools. I'll clean the bathroom in a minute, I said. I'd got red pepper on my skirt at dinner, so I wasn't overly careful as I went down on my knees to clear up the mess. Pieces of sweetcorn are so tiny. She didn't answer straight away. But then she turned her head slowly and looked down at me. That would be wonderful, she said. You're an angel. I don't know what I'd do without you. She went on staring down at me for a long time, as if she'd begun to think of something else but forgotten to shift her gaze. I smiled. She's right, I thought, we belong together like two clasped hands. I got up, threw away the bits, cleared the table, rinsed the plates, put the washing-up in the bowl, then opened the cupboard under the sink, took out the bucket and cloth and yellow Jif bottle, and went out into the bathroom. I didn't hear her get up. She must have forgotten to put her indoor shoes on.

Ivar will be at Gardermoen Airport by now, with his guitar and rucksack. I imagine him standing by the big windows watching the planes take off. He looks at his watch, turns and leans against a pillar, watching the crowds that pour out of the Airport Express, up the escalator and through the swing doors. He is looking for me.

There's a newspaper cutting on the pinboard next to the loo: The woman most in need of liberation is the woman that each man holds prisoner in his soul. There's also a poem that I've written out and pinned up there, it starts: 'Love yourself, love yourself through.' I think that's how the world works. I can't just sit and expect someone else to come and fill me with all the good feelings I need. I am responsible for myself. And I have to be the first to give. I was thinking of Ivar. Looking back, I can see how much strength I had. How happy I was. I gave thanks to Our Father, to the fount of all love. There was so much goodness around me suddenly, pouring into my life. I found myself humming a song from Christian Camp: Never alone, never alone, never alone, with the hope you gave. I opened my mouth and sang it aloud, several times. It was much too long since I'd cleaned the bathroom last, I had to scrub very hard to get rid of the grime in the corner behind the toilet.

I came out of the bathroom, my scalp sweating under my thick hair. Mum was in the lounge. She'd changed into her silk-lined Chinese dressing gown, filing the hard skin on her toes as she listened to 'I Just Called to Say I Love You', by that blind black guy whose name I forget. She didn't look at me. I put the blue bucket back under the kitchen sink, then went into my room and shut the door.

I lie on my bed now with my Bible. I always have it beside my pillow for protection at night, when it's dark. I pray for God to speak to me. I do not need comfort, O Father, I do not need help. Just give me calm, endurance and the serenity to wait. With closed eyes I open the Scriptures up at a random page and read. Psalm 77: I cry aloud to God, aloud to God, and he will hear me. In the day of my trouble I seek the Lord; in the night my hand is stretched out without wearying.

This is my room. Here I am. Inside a small cube. Floor area: six square metres. Height: three and a half metres. Twenty-one cubic metres. Under my bed are two small armchairs, bought at a jumble sale, and a round wooden table. Lying on the table are some books, novels, and beside them a candle in a broken holder. On the floor a stripy carpet. Everything in various shades of blue. Nearest me is a desk, a pine top with IKEA legs, on it my PC, an old model I got cheaply from a student on my course. On the shelf are my writing things and a sable watercolour brush. To the left of my loft bed is the window, almost filling the entire wall. I look down into the courtyard. I can't decide which is my favourite: blue or grey. There's something muted about grey, undemanding. I like it. It absorbs all the other colours into itself, takes its place at their side, is loyal. Blue, on the other hand, a luminous ultramarine, vibrates, is utterly itself, apologizes for nothing.

It was too early to leave for Mass, so I sat at my desk, searching out the tones of grey in the courtyard. It takes practice to be able to see nuances of colour. The bluish grey of the wall straight ahead, the deeper grey of the roof, and the purplish grey behind the grey-green plastic bins with their grey-black lids. I pushed my PC in towards the wall, placed the keyboard on top of it, then took down my paintbox and paper, and my old water jug. I mixed my colours in the little egg-shaped hollows in the plastic palette. I've no ambitions with my painting. I was doing this for pleasure, as a form of meditation.

Oh, so beautiful, said Mum. Suddenly she was standing behind me in the doorway, wearing a new outfit, all in grey: grey tights, iron-grey blouse, my scarf with a hint of purple-blue tied tightly around her neck. She was holding a book, her index finger keeping her place, the one I'd borrowed from the Social Sciences library about the pioneers of Gestalt therapy. She must have found it in my bag. Now she was leaning against the doorframe, wanting to read me a passage. I wasn't listening. I was watching the colours run into each other on the paper, their edges blurring. I decided I'd wait for it to dry and then go over it with pencil. *Blücher*, the German cruiser, the Battle of Drøbak Fjord, a massive explosion, Mum's hair in flames, like the burning bush. Perhaps Mum is my bush, I thought, perhaps she's the bearer of the message I'm meant to hear. An insistent buzzing sound met my ears, the doorbell. That'll be Svenn, said Mum, giving me a meaningful glance. Svenn is her friend. They visit places together, go for walks, to concerts, exhibitions, parks. Mum went to open the door. Suddenly it came over me again and I started to cry. No sobbing, just tears. Water, I thought, nothing but salt water, dropping onto the paper, making minuscule white suns. Clearly the salt had an effect on the colours, erasing them. I didn't understand what was happening inside me. Then it passed, like a rain cloud, drifting away.

I looked at the colours I had mixed. I always try to choose many shades of a single colour, then slice into it, break the colour up with something unexpected. Now they were both in my doorway. Mum and Svenn, smiling at me. They've succeeded, I thought, in each finding someone they resemble to the point of disappearing. Their sight reminded me of a development theory for the human personality: each of us is born with tendencies or traits that drive us to seek certain stimuli, and these, in turn, lead us on further, reinforcing the original traits which caused us to make our initial choices. Research was carried out on identical twins who had been raised apart. Meeting again as adults, they were often shocked at the similarity of their choices: both might have six silver rings on the left hand, the same moustache, a rose tattoo in exactly the same place on their shoulders, enjoy the same films, order the same dish at a Chinese restaurant. Svenn stroked Mum's back as he told me about an exhibition I ought to see, painting as I did. He'd been himself already, and now he'd come to see if Mum wanted to go. I'm glad for her that she has him, I think he's kind. Gentle and sensitive. He's married with four children, so they only meet now and then. I read in the *Christian Times* that if one person in a couple is a believer, both are saved, the one's faith saving the other. That got me thinking of Ivar again.

I wanted to save him. I imagined we were on a sinking ship; I stretched my hand out to him from a lifeboat and he grabbed me just in time. I had to slap my hand hard. You deserved that, Johanne. Idiotic fantasies. Mum and Svenn had gone into the lounge and closed the door. I heard the clacking of Mum's shoes. Svenn always pads about softly in socks. I went into the hall and looked on the mirror shelf. There was the envelope. I looked inside. A 100-kroner note. I began putting my outdoor clothes on. An envelope containing money is our agreed sign, a necessity when living in such a cramped space. It meant I had to stay out for a while. The money was so that I could go to a café. A 100-kroner note. I wondered why it was so much. I wanted to open the door and tell Mum she was being too generous. But I needed the money, so I didn't. You're so easily bought, Johanne. It's unprincipled. Immoral. I put the cash in my inside pocket and decided to go for a walk before going into town for Mass.

The neighbour's cat was sitting out in the courtyard. It made me think of Harlow's research with monkeys. His research would have been impossible with cats, I thought, since they seem not to have any real need for close communication. Dogs, on the other hand, are different, I mused. I went out of the front gate and crossed the street. I took a little path that rises steeply up the slope on the other side. At the top is a large house. I wandered into the garden at the back. I could look straight into our apartment, see the whole of the lounge where Mum sleeps. But I was quite far away. They were too small for me to see anything clearly. I stood for a moment on the wet lawn. It must have been raining again. There was a strange smell under that big tree, I didn't know what. A sweet, rotten odour. I saw Svenn walk through the room; he was naked. He bent down by the door, as though he was fetching something before walking back to the bed.

The pavement was wet. I crossed Riddervolds Square. I had to watch my step: the fallen leaves were slippery from the rain. I remember those leaves, particularly their yellow colour and the way they'd started to rot. I thought about Ivar. I had to try not to let him come too close. I mustn't forget my plans. My professional clinical psychology course, living with Mum during my studies so as to avoid taking out a loan, and then eventually moving into The Barns, the little development that Mum talks about building around Granny's house. A place where she and my brother and I can all live. As long as I kept to my plan, I'd manage. I stepped on something slippery and nearly fell. The soles of my shoes had worn smooth. I felt a wrench in my back and it immediately stiffened. Entering Universitetsgaten, I stayed on the side of the road with the grass verge, walking under the trees and avoiding the bookshop window displays. I was going to Mass, so I needed a clear head. I tried to get myself into a state of openness, of sensitivity and focus. Leaning my head back, I looked up at the sky. As an exercise I tried to imagine a sun.

Karin was standing on the landing with the smokers; I saw her as I came up round the bend in the staircase. She was smiling. She'd shaved off her hair, making her smile seem even bigger, her dimples more distinct. She was in a discussion with one of the boys on her theology course. Dressed in black, he had long, curly dark hair and a long dark coat, and I saw a scruffy leather-bound Bible poking out of his pocket. I realized I liked to see Karin this way, to watch her without her knowing. He noticed me coming up behind her. I knew him vaguely and he told her I was coming. She smiled again, a smile that reached out to him, then turning she ran towards me, hugged me, put her arm around me. You've got to come and back me up in this hopeless debate, she said. It's about women pastors again. She held me round the waist and together we went over. The boy and I greeted each other with a nod. How do we know, I asked, that God is a man? There are so many basic premises that are just taken for granted. Don't you have any tradition of basic critical analysis in theology? He looked at me and smiled. He seemed happy to capitulate. Karin's cheeks were flushed, her blue eyes shone, their whites pure white. More people I knew arrived; we smiled, hugged, laughed. The others started drifting into the chapel. Karin and I followed them, going in last, taking our service sheets and hymn books and sitting at the back on the creaky chairs. We were in a side chapel. The altar stood in the corner beneath the window, draped in a white cloth with a red runner, bathed in light from the little candles that were ranged along the sill behind it. The window looked out on the National Gallery. Sometimes, when there were a lot of people here, it would be open and then we could hear the passing cars on Universitetsgaten and the traffic lights bleeping for the green man.

One of the boys was playing a service prelude on the piano. The room was hushed even before he began. Then he hit a single key, the same note over and over again, until the notes started to climb, up and up, as if he was trying to reach something high above him, as though the music were made of light. I tried to enter into the music with my whole self. Tried to see God in the light that I could hear in the music. Father, I thought, where can we find You if not here? Then it occurred to me that I shouldn't look at all. The point wasn't to find. All I had to do was open myself up and God would come. Just *be*, I thought. In the here and now. Then it came over me again. But there was nothing bad about it this time, no tears, just a sense of sadness, perfect stillness, emptiness, like a gentle blessing. I didn't put anything in the collection box. I had a 100-kroner note in my inside pocket, but I gave nothing.

It's my fault. Or maybe it's a punishment for having sex outside marriage and it's God keeping me here at home. I ought to be furious, smash the window, hammer on the walls. That's what they do in films, they react, they let it out. I'm not sure why I don't. Perhaps I find it hard to express my anger. Or maybe I've too much wisdom; I see the situation from every perspective and then anger appears unnecessary, unreasonable, child-ish – egotistical.

Karin looked up from the table and smiled at me with cream on her top lip. We hadn't stayed for refreshments after Mass, we'd gone to a café instead – naughty really, since being the positive, resourceful girls we were, we had some responsibility for the social scene down there. I felt bad. We went Dutch on the hot chocolate. I should have treated Karin but didn't. Johanne thinks only of herself. Karin stroked the soft stubble at the back of her head, tugged at the earrings in her right ear and smiled as she told me about the job she'd been offered as a stand-in pastor outside Trondheim next summer. I imagined her in her robes with that shaved head. They'll be in for a shock. She told me I had to visit her. I said Mum and I were planning a trip to England. Your mother's so nice, she said. I told her how easy it was living with Mum, like being in a collective, that she was my best friend. Apart from you, I said, smiling. We sat in silence for a moment, eyes meeting tenderly, heads inclined. The music in that café, the melodious instrumentals, I can hear them now, making me feel as though it happened long ago, as though years had passed since we sat there, instead of just two weeks. My song. I asked her about the boy she'd been talking to when I arrived. She described how, during a lecture, he'd suddenly got up and made a furious statement before marching out. We both laughed at the self-importance of young men. She's in love, I thought. I was suddenly aware of how much I liked her, how happy

I was to be sitting here with her. Just as I always felt joy when I knelt beside her to take Holy Communion, her arm touching mine. For a split second I saw right inside her left ear; it had a fantastic lustre. You're going to look great in your robes, I said. She couldn't wait, she said, for the sense of ritual, for leading the ceremony. A celebration of God. To be able to stand at the altar after the postlude, stretching her arms out and saying, 'Go in peace, to love and serve the Lord.'

Shall we go for a walk? I asked. Thinking back now, it was as though there was a motor in my body that had been set in motion, running uncontrollably; I wasn't the one making decisions. Karin agreed. She got up, talking about the sedentariness of student life, her bad back, all the exercises she had to do. I knew where we'd go. Of course. I stood up too and put my coat on. I had to bend my knees and go down with a straight back to pick up my bag from the floor. It was a damp evening, but mild, so I felt less guilty for luring Karin out on an evening walk, the motive for which she could not suspect. We headed towards Bislett. My aim was to go to the top of St Hanshaugen to look out over the town and be close to God, before walking back down towards Gamle Aker. It might bring us luck, good fortune, and then perhaps we might meet him. This isn't like you, Johanne, said Karin, laughing, you're generally in bed by five past ten. I smiled. There's so much you don't know, Karin, I thought. So much I can't tell you. If I did, it would evaporate, lose all energy, become flat and ordinary, a thing one just talks about with a friend. This is my everything. My whole life. When a thing isn't put into words, it can't be destroyed. So it's better to keep it inside.

We were climbing up to the reservoir at the top of the park. Suddenly we broke into a race, leaping up the steps, chests filling with air, mouths gaping. My throat rasped. Fitness, Johanne, I thought, and then I remembered a story I'd heard about women being raped with a sandpaper condom as a punishment. Karin won. We looked at each other and laughed. She was so strong, her back so straight, her head held so high, and such beautiful, clear skin. We stood at the top and the reservoir, with its floor decorated with children's drawings, lay spread below us. We turned as one and looked out. Karin took my hand and we gazed over the city. Then we went down towards Gamle Aker. Neither of us said anything. Karin seemed almost shy.

I looked up and down the street at every single crossroads. There was no one. We reached the church. It was softly illuminated. Karin was talking about an injustice that had occurred at the institute. I wasn't following. With my back to the church, I was scanning all the apartments that might overlook the square. A voice called from a window. I jumped. It was a man's voice. Karin wanted to go in the churchyard and sit on one of the benches by the wall. I heard footsteps on the narrow gravel path behind us. I turned. There he was. Ivar. A guitar case in one hand and a large bag in the other. I was suddenly frightened that he might be leaving, going away. That I'd never see him again. I could think of nothing else, as Karin talked on. Johanne, she said, tugging at my arm. I was just looking at Ivar. He'd been staring at the ground, but now he was looking straight at me, only at me. He drew closer, then came right up to us, he had to, if he was going to come past. He stopped. I said hello; my voice sounded much too weak and hoarse. He said hello back; his voice was deeper and warmer than I'd remembered. I wanted Karin to let go of my arm and for him to walk on beside me, for the two of us to go on together. In some unknown apartment he would take my face in his hands and gaze at me, look into my eyes and say that he loved me, that we belonged together, that he'd waited so long, that he'd longed for a girl, and that girl was me, and that he would look after me. And we'd lock the doors and talk all night, and he'd hold my face in his hands. I could see it all. It would be as though the rest of my body would disappear, he would love me like this, love my eyes, my face, me. Nobody would know where I was, he would hit me, slap me across the cheek, my arms, blue marks would appear instantly, and he'd call me a pussy-licker because I was with another girl when he met me, he'd make me cry and cower in a corner, before comforting me and using my body. Red velvet sofa and raw music, heavy rock, a loud bass, so loud nobody would hear his blows or my cries. There was complete silence for a moment. An eternity. Then he smiled, frowned as if he was wondering, or about to say something, but then he walked straight on. Why? Did I mean nothing to him? Two cars approached, one after the other, their lights flooding our faces. Karin looked as if she'd burst into luminous flames. Ivar was gone. I was suddenly aware of the traffic, the hum of the city – we were inside a machine. Karin stared at me strangely. I felt she was reproaching me for something. I started thinking of what to say when she made the accusations; that I'd betrayed her or shut her out. My back was so stiff it hurt; it was agony just to lift my knees. We set off towards Ullevålsveien. All I wanted was to turn back and run after him. I was sure he'd understand. Those eyes seemed to understand everything, the whole of me. Like Jesus: Rise and follow me. Oh really, Johanne! Karin was hard, almost disdainful. Who was that? she asked, as though he was that dreadful. Not all men, I wanted to say, are abusive. Some guy who works in the university canteen, I said. His name is Ivar, but I don't really know him. We've only talked briefly before today, although he's worked there since the beginning of term. I told her about the towel. I wanted her to understand the importance of this story, its secrets, its corners; I hoped its subtleties and details would come through in my voice and become a tangible reality. I saw the story of the meeting between Ivar and me as a winding forest path, losing itself in the shadow of the trees, where the air is heavy with the scent of wild flowers and nobody can tell what might happen at the next turn.

I don't think Karin saw anything special in Ivar. At least she didn't mention it. He probably wasn't good enough for her. A canteen worker. That certainly didn't match her criteria; she only ever fell in love with academics, mainly conceited theology students, once a physicist with a scholarship. She wanted me to walk her down to the station. And I should have, after she'd come all this way with me. I owed her that much, but my encounter with Ivar had made me careless and uncaring. I wanted to be alone with my longing. I said I was tired and had to get home and go to bed. We said our goodbyes at the next crossroads: Go in peace. A hug, a smile, a wave. I crossed over to the path that runs by the palace gardens, under the big trees. It struck me how much I enjoyed being alone like this. I was contented. The rain had stopped for a while now and the water had left dark patches on the asphalt, making an uneven pattern. Here and there a street lamp winked in a puddle. Ivar's eyes. I winked back.

Ivar. He's standing at a coffee bar now, waiting. The screen says Go to Gate. The flight attendant has lowered her red-lipsticked mouth to the microphone for the last call and her voice echoes through the large hall. He starts to run. Long, soft strides over flagstones and parquet. The word Boarding is flashing on the screen. Do you see it, Ivar? Do you perhaps think the letters beat with the same rhythm as my heart?

There's a song I made up when I was a child and afraid of the dark. I used to sing it as I ran home. I'd count the number of windows I passed before the song finished and then start it over again. I used to pretend the song had no end, like a bubble, a perfect sphere, and so long as I was inside it, I was safe. I kneel in front of the armchair now and bend my back as low as I can, bow my head, fold my hands. Then I sing my song several times over, without stop.

The apartment was silent and in darkness when I let myself in. It smelt of smoke and something else, sweet, peculiar. It was only about eleven or eleven thirty. I wondered if Mum had gone out with Svenn. I walked through the lounge, to the curtain that divides her room off, and looked towards the big bed by the wall. The bedclothes lay in a bundle, making it impossible to see if there was anybody under them. Mum, I said quietly. No answer. I said it again. The duvet shifted, noises came from by the wall, it was thrown aside and Mum sat bolt upright, as though she'd been disturbed by a piercing siren. She rubbed her eyes. She was wearing her pink nightdress.

What's the time? she asked. About eleven, I said. She turned towards the shelf on the wall, switched the little lamp on, found her glasses, checked her watch, took out a book and plumped the pillows up behind her. She shot me a glance over her reading glasses before opening her book, wondering perhaps if I had more to say. I saw she was halfway through one of those Swedish pocket editions. Göran Tunström, maybe. I turned and went into the bathroom, sat on the toilet with my eyes closed. When it's late I pretend I'm already asleep. I thought about the sight experiments carried out on kittens. During the first months of their lives they were put in an environment where they were exposed only to horizontal lines. As a result they failed to develop any ability to see vertical lines. The hypothesis was that a lack of visual stimulus at key sensitive periods would hinder the development of important connections between the eye and brain, despite genetic potential. I opened my eyes and saw the lilac wallpaper, the blue walls around the bath, the black-and-white-striped shower curtain. I could hear Mum's voice from the lounge, but not the words – the dividing curtain muffled the sound and I'd closed the toilet door. I wiped myself, got up and opened the door with my trousers down. Mum was walking towards me with her big round glasses on her nose, wearing her slippers from Granny and the old shawl I'd bought at a jumble sale over her shoulders. A man rang, she said. A short while ago. She looked at me with anxious eyes magnified behind her glasses. He said his name was Ivar. She spoke in a deliberate tone, as though she was warning me of some danger and wanted me to take everything in. I was suddenly gripped by fear. How had he found my number? She leant on the doorframe and watched me as I pulled up my knickers and trousers, did up the zip. Have you put on weight? she said. I turned to the tap, washed my hands meticulously. You've got my body, Mum said. The wide hips, the big knees. Karin sends her love, I said. My thoughts were on his voice: it had been here, on the telephone. Men find that irresistible, Mum said, a broad backside. Her brow was furrowed, as if she was thinking of something in particular. I cleaned my teeth with my right hand and stroked her hair with my left. It was dry at the ends. She ought to get it trimmed. Karin's a bit… said Mum. A bit what? I said. Well… she said. Go on, say it, I said. She's a bit… slow, isn't she? said Mum. She took my hand and held it against her cheek. I smiled with the toothbrush still in my mouth. She squeezed my hand and sighed, then, keeping a tight hold of it, she looked at me seriously: This Ivar, Johanne, are you sure he's right for you? Remember how relieved you were last time you got rid of that admirer of yours? Wouldn't it be daft to get yourself involved again so soon? I didn't know what to say. It wasn't true that I'd been glad last time, that wasn't how it had been. I'd never had a real boyfriend. I'd been in love, yes, last spring, with a post-grad economics student. We'd collided on the stairs, his books had scattered everywhere – macroeconomy – he'd smiled at me and our hands had met as we picked them up, like in a film, magical. I'd told her about it. Mum and I have agreed that she'll approve any future husband. Her experience will prevent me from marrying a man who lacks boundaries, self-control and sensitivity. The social economist disappeared. I saw him in the canteen a few times, nothing more. I was sad, that's how I see it now. I'd had so many ideas about how things might turn out. I studied for my exams like crazy, and did well, better than ever. I expect that's what Mum remembered, the excitement over my end-of-term results. But it was she who was most pleased. And now I didn't know what to say to her, it was all turning into a jumble, a fog in my head. I felt a pressure behind my forehead, in my eyebrow. Exhaustion, no doubt, after a long week of studies. Suddenly I was gripped by fear. Perhaps she was right. Perhaps Ivar was dangerous, a bad man, cold, manipulative, abusive. That look in his eyes, could I really trust it? And now he had my telephone number, he could easily find out where I lived. My back felt stiff. Mum took my hand, squeezed it again, and stroked it with her other hand. I looked at her nail polish, several layers thick. My dear, sweet Johanne, she said, the best girl in the whole world. Then, after giving my hand a final squeeze, she let it go and went back to bed. I closed the bathroom door, turned back to the mirror, spat into the sink, rinsed my mouth, then stared at myself, trying to find any concrete reason for anybody loving me. I thought about the development of babies' sight. They seek contrasts between light and dark, and see best from about thirty centimetres away, the distance from the breast to the mother's face. While the baby feeds, it studies its mother's eyebrows, hairline and eyes, because those are the areas of greatest contrast. In my bed I lay straight out: I get to sleep fastest that way, flat on my back without a pillow, arms at my sides, like a mummy or dead child. I sank down and down, falling into a deep sleep, and as I was sinking I thought: Forgive me, Lord. Forgive me and bless me. When I was a child I used to think of something I was looking forward to, then concentrate all my thoughts onto that one thing. I remember wondering, on that Friday night, what I was looking forward to. What, Johanne, are you looking forward to? Through the wall I could hear the thudding of the bass, with the occasional solitary note or line of melody. Mum's Walkman. She often turns up the volume and puts it on the shelf, so as not to have the headphones pressing against her ears.

I lie on the floor of my room and look out at the sky. It's dark grey now. A pair of pigeons have made their nest under the eaves. There's an occasional flurry of activity, when they flit back and forth. I'd been looking forward to flying with Ivar. I didn't tell him: it seemed such a daft thing to look forward to, so banal, sitting there next to each other, strapped into our seats, holding hands at take-off, leaning towards the window together, peering down at the ground, with the sensation that we could see everything. I imagine him next to another girl now, with short blonde hair and green eyes, older than me, more experienced. She gives him a lopsided smile. Karin's teeth. Karin ought to have stood by me more, I think to myself. Why don't I have friends who are there when it really counts? I want to slap Karin, standing there in her pastor's gown, holding her hands out. Smack her round the face. Swing my fists into those big tits, so the chalice spills and the Communion wafers scatter.

I remember lying in bed. It was a Saturday morning, a clear autumn day, blue sky, sunshine, I had the duvet right up to my chin. I'm always happier in the morning, my mind is lighter. I tried to concentrate on all the things I was looking forward to: passing my foundation-year exams with such good grades that I'd get straight onto the Professional Psychology Programme. Passing my finals with flying colours so I can pick and choose jobs, combine research with practice, practice and theory. And when Granny dies and The Barns are built, I'll have my own practice in light, elegant premises. I'll have long, interesting conversations with Mum. And have an older, professionally experienced mentor in town with whom I can meet on occasion. An elderly man perhaps, with warm eyes and a beard. I'll plant trees all the way to the entrance of my office, so my clients can walk through an avenue of birches. Going into therapy is a kind of journey: it's important to attend to the aesthetics and bring as much beauty to the experience as possible. I felt how the thought of all these things rippled like energy through my body. I imagined my mentor with his big, shaggy beard. We were in his office, I was sitting on his desk, he had a huge belly, I wore a short, thin summer dress. He pulled my knickers down and held his big warm hands around my waist, he bent down and began to lick me. I leant back, felt his beard between my thighs, his moustache prickling the top of my cunt, it tingled when I thought of it. I wanted him to come inside me, my body was an empty space that needed to be filled to exist, he had to come inside for me to know I was here. I pretended that I'd done this before, that I knew what to do. I imagined lying there and wanting it, letting this man who knew what to do do it. He undid the big buckle on the belt of his soft canvas trousers, tugged it out and let it fall to the floor, stood up to his desk, between my legs. And I looked at him as he dropped his trousers and boxer shorts so they slid down his calves. I could see his swollen penis, so large that it protruded from under his shirt and belly, and I had to smile. I put my feet up on the desk and opened my thighs as wide as I could, pushed against him. Come inside me, I said. I imagined that his body and mine fitted together in a unique way, so that even when he moved he was close, rubbing and fucking me simultaneously. I ran my fingers over my body, touching myself. Some people say it's a sin to masturbate. If so, forgive me, Father. He pulled out of me and picked up the belt, his expression changed, his eyes filled with anger, he started to beat me with the left hand as he entered me again, hard, raw. He raised the hand that held the thick belt. I assumed Mum was in the bathroom, probably on the toilet, smoking. I had to be careful not make a noise. I tried to bring back the nice images. Every time I do this, it seems to get nasty and twisted. Suddenly my body started to shake: I imagined my mentor had stuck a big finger up my arse, I trembled all over.

I lay on my side with my head on the pillow and looked out of the window; the blue of the sky was so clear it almost hurt. I felt it come again. I didn't cry much, just a few tears rolling down, wetting my eyes. I wondered about the cause. My thoughts lay embedded in sinews and skin, beyond my reach. Those of you who believe yourselves to be clean, without sin, without guilt, may cast the first stone. I saw myself under a heap of stones. What would it be like to be stoned? What would it be like to experience such pain? Would you feel every individual stone, with a pause between each one, or would it be a single endless avalanche? Would they follow one another so closely as to form one line of pain, a single unbroken streak?

The really stupid thing about this door is its loose handle. I can't tug at it, because it'll fall off and I can't put it back on from inside. I've told Mum we should fix it. Perhaps these psychology studies are a waste of time. Perhaps I ought to do something practical, study a craft, learn how to repair things, make myself useful. I need a pee. I wonder if I'll get out soon so I can go to the toilet. This is ridiculous, Johanne. But it's no fun being locked in. Not today, when I was meant to go off travelling and things. You'd be too late now, Johanne. And as I say it word by word I can hear that it is true, like ripping off a plaster. I always arrive too late for anything important. It's as though this thought were the key to another door, the door to a chamber of tears, and everything behind it starts to pour out. I lie on my back on the floor and let the tears flow. I'm alone here and there's no one to see. They trickle to the sides and down towards my ears, leaving my cheeks dry. What a weird way to cry. I have to smile at myself. I take a lock of my hair and make it into a brush to sweep away the wetness.

The day after I met Ivar, Mum and I spent Saturday in our usual way. I linked my arm in hers as we walked past the palace across the sandy gravel square and started the long slope down to Karl Johan. A chilly day, light and clear and deep green; in places the leaves had turned yellow and here and there red. A pale, white dust began to cover our four shoes; I remember looking down at them, we walked in step. I saw myself as a child, marching up to the palace on Constitution Day. For two consecutive years, I'd joined the other young hopefuls behind the brass band, wearing the little sidecap and pleated blue skirt that cost too much, a music case dangling at my thigh. I abandoned music classes before I was ever given an instrument. Mum stopped and took out her camera. Can I trouble you to take my picture? she asked. Checking her hair, she positioned herself before the palace and told me I must try to include some greenery. I asked how she wanted to look, serious or smiling. I just want to be beautiful, she said. I studied her through the lens. She seemed so small in the viewfinder. I moved closer to get more light on her face. Then clicked. She put the camera away and took out a packet of cigarettes, found her lighter, then stood, for a long time, holding her unlit cigarette, gazing out over the tall trees into the distance. Perhaps, I thought, she wants me to move out. She's decided it's too expensive to have me living with her. I'm just a nuisance. Perhaps she's thinking of what she could do with all the money I spend on food. I didn't want her to be angry with me. It was Saturday. I wanted her to be happy and for us to do all the usual things. I didn't want any changes, not now, not in the middle of term. I stroked her hair. It's permissible to protect oneself, to guard oneself, I had to allow her that much. She must keep her secrets for herself. She brushed my hand off, I don't think it was conscious, then puffed her hair up with her fingers as though I'd flattened it. You drifted off completely, I said. Oh, did I? she said, lighting her cigarette. You're often rather distant, I said. Really? At work I'm constantly hearing how focused I am. Present in the moment. A frown appeared on her brow, as though she were pondering over what she'd said. We started to walk again. I didn't know what to say, my head felt empty. It scares me that I can be so vacant. My brain should be more active. I tried to remember any independent ideas I'd come up with lately, the thought I always have, for example, when I go through my developmental psychology book, see Harlow's pictures of baby monkeys and think this isn't science but art. It is true but also false. It's a lie, yet it gives us fresh insight into something we all know and recognize. The importance of these experiments isn't to be found in any report, in words or phrases, but in those pictures, in our memory of them: the face of that tiny ape, its huge eyes and the piece of terry cloth that is its 'mother'. I felt it come again, the tears welling up. I tried to think of something else so Mum wouldn't notice. What's happening? I thought, I don't trust myself, I've no self-control. I decided I was probably hungry. Erratic blood sugar levels, that must be it.

We went into Tanum bookshop as usual. I can't understand why I always get hungry this early on a Saturday. I'd been thinking of food almost before we left home.

Mum was looking for the paperback edition of a book my brother had recommended. He's studying in the US, but does office work during his vacations here in town and sleeps on a mattress in the lounge. He left in August. It'll be months before I see him again. I looked at Mum. She'd already found two books she wanted. We were standing on the landing where they keep the English paperbacks. I've been thinking... She stopped. Her mouth dropped open. I followed her gaze. She was gawping at a young couple standing below us by the travel guides and maps. The man had round glasses and a mop of dark hair. He was telling the girl something, and she was listening intently, her head tilted, nodding. She was equally attractive, with long blonde hair and a symmetrical face, like a doll. What? I said. I glanced at Mum again, then tried to find a book I'd heard about on the shelves behind her. She didn't answer and went on staring. Mum! I said, nudging her arm discreetly. She frowned, as if her thoughts were scattered about in her brain and she needed the muscles in her forehead to gather them up. There's something about men, she said, something... She stopped. I registered my own relief. But Mum was still watching them. I looked again too. The girl smiled with beautiful even, white teeth, and he gave her a lingering smile before continuing to talk, I assumed they were planning a trip, a weekend in Berlin perhaps. What is it? I said. It's just... there's something wrong with them. She shifted her gaze towards me. Men are so simple. Controlled by sex and power. Like robots, she said. What do you mean? I said. She fixed her eyes on me seriously, but said nothing, then went back to the shelves, wrapped up, it seemed, in her own thoughts and determined to focus on them without interference. I went down the little staircase and wandered about a bit, before stopping to browse through the gardening books near the tills. I have to focus on textbooks in term time, so I tend to avoid the fiction section in case I find anything too interesting. Besides, books are expensive and I'm trying to save as much as possible for the future. Mum arrived with an armful of books. She rolled her eyes, so I'd see how she despaired at herself. We went to a till and while she paid I looked at the art cards. Then we went to the French patisserie on the first floor and found a smoking table with a red-checked tablecloth. What would you like? Mum asked, as we approached the glass counter of croissants and glazed fruit tarts. I'll have to look first, I said. It's so rare for me to spend money eating out that when I do get the chance I can never make up my mind. She whispered that I could have anything I wanted and pointed at the purse in her right hand with her left middle finger. I noticed how like Granny's her hands were. I stared down at my own. I may be young now, I thought, but it all lies hidden in there. Some day the family line will reveal itself in my fingers too. I'll be sitting with a client perhaps and I'll see Mum in my hands. My mind will wander and I'll lose focus on what my client is saying. Somebody on my course told me that his psychologist had fallen asleep once when he was in therapy. But he still went on seeing the man. If it had happened to me as a client, I wouldn't have told a soul. Going to therapy would probably be educational for me, but my conscience won't let me take a place from someone who really needs it. Actually this guy is pretty weird. I really don't understand how his mind works.

I carried our tray over to the table. Mum went back to the counter for cutlery and serviettes. She was muttering irritably about a remark the man behind the counter had made. So unfriendly, she said, it spoils the ambience. But still, we'll have a nice time now, won't we, darling? She smiled to herself as she lifted my plate and double espresso from the tray and onto the table. She took out her copy of *Dagbladet*, pulled out the centre section and handed me the rest. She leafed through to the main interview and started to read it as she took huge bites out of her roll. I studied her face: the open pores, the slack skin under her chin, the thin lips. According to one of our psychology books, we develop only in close relationships. Only in intimate relationships do we expose ourselves to the possibility of change, to things being set in motion. I went straight to the culture pages. There was a review of the Swedish novel that had come out recently in translation. Mum and I had gone to a free reading, arranged in conjunction with the launch. Svenn was at home with his family and couldn't come. All I remember about this book is that a man baked a cake, sat in a café and lied to a woman, convinced her he was dying. Mum and I were both infuriated by the complete absence of beauty in his book. She wanted to go, but I wanted to stay and listen anyway. Eventually Mum got up and left me there on my own. It was early autumn, so it was still quite light in the evenings, and I remember thinking I'd be safe getting home. During the interval, I bought a large coffee and a pastry that had doubtless sat on the counter all day; not that it crossed my mind at the time, and I had enough money even though Mum had gone and she's usually the one who pays when we go out. The author came up to me after the reading. He asked why my mother had left. I wondered how he knew she was my mother. Well, you look so alike, he said with a smile. He sat down and wanted me to talk. So, he said, tell me about yourself. I told him I was studying psychology. He laughed. I liked him. He seemed so honest. I wanted to say something impressive, so he'd remember me. I talked about a subject that's often on my mind, the idea that we have to come close to people for change to take place. Other girls came over to our table and talked to him, but although he answered them, his gaze was fixed on me. We went on talking for a while. Then he got up to go to the toilet, but never returned. I remember trying not to be upset. Maybe that's the way artists are, they get a sudden impulse, an idea maybe. It wasn't too late, so I walked home. It was a waste of money to take the tram when it wasn't essential. When I got back home I told Mum that I'd talked to the author. We often sit in the kitchen in the evening and chat, Mum with a Diet Coke, me with a cup of tea. She said it was dangerous to get involved with strange men. Imagine, Johanne, if you and I weren't living together and you'd taken him home. Taking a man back is like entering a contract, promising him something. Just think what he could have done with you. There are more dangerous men out there than you'd believe, Johanne. They're a danger to women when they think they're going to get something. That's why we carry alarms, isn't it? But once you've taken them into your apartment, there's not a lot you can do. What if he'd tied you up? Had a knife in his jacket? He could have done anything he wanted. Absolutely anything, Johanne. She was scaring me now. The sweat ran cold under my arms. I was relieved nothing had happened. To think we might have gone for a walk in the park. For days I pictured what could have taken place, it would flood into my head as I sat in the reading room or in a lecture, like a gigantic unexpected wave on the beach that you barely leap back from in time. I don't know how I'd get by without Mum. I looked across at her. She'd returned to her newspaper. Was leafing through it. I looked down at my knees under my long brown skirt. Then I felt it come. A note, a single piercing tone inside my head. Suddenly the café seemed to go completely quiet, the lounge music from the piano downstairs melted away; the people at the tables started grimacing, but it was impossible to hear what they said. Perhaps the air was stale in here, with so many people right under the roof. I asked if we might leave. I could barely hear my own voice; the volume button on the loudspeaker must be out of order, there was no filter, no electrical contact, just tables and chairs being overturned in the distance. I've got some reading I need to do at home, I said, standing up. I have over thirty pages to read this week.

I'm desperate for a pee. I have a wastepaper bin, a square, steel bucket. If I don't get out soon, I'll have to pee in it. It's not a big deal, worse things happened during the war. They had to pee in the same bowl they got their food and water in. Piss out; water in. I packed my textbooks last night, so they're out in the hall in my case, together with three dresses, clean knickers and a pair of shoes for all weathers. My method notes are still in here though, right in front of me, in their purple clip file. I could apply myself to them properly now and not, as I usually do, give up halfway through. Then at least I'd have achieved something while I was stuck in here. Validity and reliability. Reliability is a technical matter, measurable, testable. Validity is, by contrast, a more complex problem that I don't feel I can even scrape the surface of. For example, the process of generalization: the transference of results obtained in a small, artificial experiment on the assumption that they will be applicable in a wider, real-life context. But more fraught still, is the notion of conceptual validity: to what extent is the concept you're examining – for example, happiness – truly covered by your investigation? In order to know that, you have to give a definition of happiness, which means you've already decided what happiness is, in which case your experiment is rendered completely invalid: a construct. It therefore seems impossible to get a fresh understanding of the concept, or to discover anything fundamentally new about it. And once conceptual validity is threatened, the entire experiment falls apart and you will have investigated the wrong thing. I feel nauseous. I have layer upon layer of thoughts in my head and the bottom one has nothing to grip on to. I should open the window, the air in here is so stale. I sleep with the door closed at night and it's been closed all morning. I look at the door handle, at the keyhole. I stare at them so minutely that they seem unreal, expanding, morphing, suddenly appearing soft and malleable, about to melt and trickle down. It must be the bad air in here. I should open the window, but I don't want to ask for help. Opening it will signal that I've given up. It'll make it apparent that I want to get out. But you do want to get out, Johanne! Yes, I do, but not like that. I don't want to ask for anything. Then I'll be forever bound. I want to manage on my own.

The ticking of the alarm clock is suddenly so distinct. I clamber up onto the loft bed and fetch it down. I sit on the floor with my back against the door, holding it in both hands. Small and white, it reminds me of an egg, with the sound of a chick inside it, wanting to get out. Tapping, tapping with its beak. I've seen them on TV in close-up. Easter chicks, like little yellow fluff-balls.

Jesus's tomb was like an egg too. He was the chick that hatched from it. He fought his way out for our sins and to set us free.

I was standing in the hall. The church bells were ringing, I stood quietly listening to their mighty clang as the sound came in through the open lounge window. It was sunny, quite mild. Strange to think it was only eleven days ago. I usually leave home when they ring for the second time. That means it's half past, so I won't have to stress. I have time to say hi and talk a bit if I see anyone I know, or just take my seat near the second pillar from the back, along the right-hand wall, and focus my mind. Mum was in the shower. She usually comes to the palace chapel too, even though the services are primarily aimed at members of the Oslo Student Church Association. We could have left together, but she wasn't ready, and since I hate being late I gave up waiting. She'd have to take responsibility for herself. I knocked on the bathroom door as soon as the bells had stopped and I was dressed; in shades of brown, perfect for an autumn Sunday. Hurry up, I said. She didn't answer. I knocked again. Mum, I said. Yes, all right, she said. I'm leaving now, I said.

The trees in the palace gardens were so beautiful, the sight of them produced a lump in my stomach. I remember thinking this was the place to come with a broken heart. Ivar drifted into my mind and I smiled. Somehow I was already pining for him, feeling a sense of loss. Perhaps life sends us signs. Warns us. I walked past the little duck pond on the left. To my right was Queen's Park, already closed for the year, the lake drained long ago. I walked up the slope and came out alongside the palace. It is shady there in the morning. A group had gathered around the door. I didn't know them well, but recognized two of them as committee members of the Student Congregation. They borrow the chapel in the palace basement and always manage a full house. We exchanged smiles as I passed them on my way in. A couple of boys were wearing traditional knickerbockers and trainers, their rucksacks on the gravel beside them.

I went down the little staircase. A pure white sunlight was pouring in through the latticed windows of the inner palace courtyard. The marble gleamed. The materials were all so beautiful in here. Terje from the theology college was standing beside a table handing out hymn books and service sheets. It would be High Mass today, with a procession and incense. I gave him a hug and asked how he was feeling. So far only a few people had come down. Generally there's a rush in the last ten minutes and then it gets quite rowdy, but right now it was quiet. He told me the subcommittee had gone through some important issues relating to the institute. Terje is a star student, with an amazing grasp of theology, and always so friendly. Karin's mentioned some of the Bible interpretations he's put forward at seminars, impressive exegeses. He even has a liberal opinion on women pastors. I gave him a questioning glance. Ah, *that*, he said. Hmm, no change there, I'm afraid. Terje lives with a fear that everything might disappear. These days, he said, whenever I cycle to college I have to stare at the ground, because I'm sure there'll be a crack or a massive crater. And if I don't keep looking down, my bike might plunge headlong, taking me with it. At night I dream I'm being smashed against the hard, craggy edges of this hole as I fall. I scream for help, but nobody hears. Hello there, God! Terje raised his eyes to the ceiling. I followed his gaze. The ceiling was painted a light blue with wispy little white clouds. Our eyes met. Well, at least it makes me wear a helmet. He laughed. I tried to picture the hole he'd described. It must be awful. Perhaps it's Freudian, I thought. Perhaps you need a woman, a caring woman who'll listen. For all I knew, he'd never had a partner either. Well, I said, it would have been nice to receive an answer! It was a bit stuffy in there already, how would it be in an hour's time with over 200 people? The congregation was streaming in now, coming in behind Terje, waiting for hymn books. I had to hurry if I was going to secure the seat I wanted. See you then, I said. He stared at me as he carried on handing out the hymn books, and without looking down at what he was doing, he smiled and told me he was happy I'd come. I felt like hugging him. I gave him a little wave, before turning to walk on. My body was filled with a warmth after talking to him, as though he was a brother. This was where I belonged. In my Father's house. All I had to do now was find a seat near the wall at the back, from where I'd be able to see both the pulpit and the altar. I like to sit straight in front of the pulpit, so it feels as if the pastor is talking to me. Of course he's talking to you, I said to myself. He's talking to everyone. He's the wisest pastor I know. Whenever he takes the service I have this feeling in my stomach that everything he says is true. I found my seat, took off my jacket and sat down. I closed my eyes. I felt the warmth of the sun, of the congregation filling the chapel. The seats were taken on either side of me. There were people everywhere. I liked it. Then suddenly it went quiet and I heard a boy's voice, a fragile song, chanting, faint at first, far away, and then moving closer. I opened my eyes. The procession was on its way. At the front was the pastor carrying a mace or some kind of rod, behind him a chubby theology student in white robes, swinging a censer, and behind him again the chorister, a tiny boy with blond, almost white, hair. I caught just the occasional glimpse of him between all the rows of pews and bodies. I wished he would never stop singing. I wanted to take him home with me and look after him. Perhaps he's an orphan, I thought. The theology student and he sat on either side of the altar, facing each other. I could see him clearly from where I was. He looked so beautiful, so delicate, as though he might break at any moment. The pastor welcomed everybody. I imagined the boy was my son. We'd gone to the seaside and I watched over him while he swam. Then we ran along the water's edge, jostling one another, splashing, laughing, and he cut himself on a shell and bled and cried, and I comforted him, held him close and sang into his ear so only he could hear. And without a word, he knew I loved him.

During the reading, which the theology student took, someone came in, letting the door close with a slam, and I heard the sound of shoes coming down the stone steps. Mum. I looked towards the entrance of the chapel. She'd dyed her hair. So that was what she'd been up to when I left. She was wearing her verdigris imitation fur and it gleamed against the copper colour of her hair. She was looking up at the altar. From the moment she'd come into view, her eyes were turned upwards. Looking at the pastor. Staring at him. I'd suggested she should be more discreet, but she hadn't listened. Terje crept over and handed her a hymn book and service sheet. His own, no doubt, since with so many people they must have run out long ago. She gave him a fleeting smile, before focusing again on the pastor. Finding an empty seat at the back, she sat down and leant against the wall. I turned again to the altar. I tried to forget she was there and to remember what I'd been thinking before she arrived.

I am sitting next to Edward. He is grinning, showing his broken tooth. My front teeth have just started to come through. Mum and Dad stand behind us. All four of us are smiling out of a grainy black and white photograph in the Parish Newsletter: The congregation's family of the month. Ready for the forest ramble. Happy and sociable. I remembered a man who cried when he received Communion. He sat four pews in front of us, tears rolling down his cheeks. I thought he must have committed an awful crime, since he was so relieved to be saved.

Whenever the pastor spoke I felt important, of value, as though he'd placed a glowing rock inside me that warmed my whole body. When the time came to take Holy Communion I waited for the others to empty the pew before taking my place in the queue for the altar, and joining in the hymn, so beautiful, so familiar, filling the chapel, weaving among us, and everyone sang, without stop, until all those who wanted to had been up to the pastor and received the bread and wine. On my way back, I passed Mum. She always waits until the very end. She grabbed me by the arm. Wasn't that a beautiful sermon? *So* beautiful? She spoke slowly, giving every word equal weight, and looked at me, eyes gleaming. Suddenly I couldn't remember a thing the pastor had said. It was completely gone. My head was empty. The rock had lost its warmth. I felt a tightening in my eyebrow, I wanted to get back to my seat, I was blocking the aisle. I nodded. Yes, I said. I stroked her cheek cursorily, before continuing, slipping behind the back pew and round to the chairs along the side. And white light spilt in from the palace courtyard.

She looks at the bars on the window. At the patterns that form across the floor as the sun moves. Later, afterwards, she gazes into the street below. With her chain pulled out as far as it will go, she stands at the window and looks down on the dust, the bodies, the traffic. The small boy has sung a brief, melancholy song. A hymn set to an old folk tune. The procession has passed from the altar and down the aisle. When he disappears into the backroom, I thought, he'll be tied to the radiator, his tunic yanked up under his belly. He is singing this plaintive song to send us a message. In the hope we'll decipher its meaning. I tried to think of something else, but the film was rolling unstoppably in my head. A tight little-boy-hole. The chapel doesn't have a bell, so there's silence when the service is finished. Complete silence. I tried to think about something else. I looked at the pastor's back. He was tall, slender, dark. Mum often talked about him after church, as we walked home arm in arm. He has wise eyes. I can see why she's drawn to him. And, like Ivar, when he wears white it emphasizes his eyes even more and they look really large. I had to smile at myself for thinking about him in those terms. God! Whoops. I said it aloud. Someone turned and looked at me.

All I had to do was keep to my plan, I thought, and everything would fall into place. But I'm not so sure now. I should bang on the door, open the window and yell out into the backyard so they hear me. But what should I say? That I'm locked in? They'll think I'm mad. They'll call the emergency psychiatric unit, if, that is, they can be bothered. I think about Kitty Genovese, attacked by a madman as she walked home from work at three in the morning in Kew Gardens, New York. Thirty-eight neighbours heard her cries and watched from their windows, but not a single person called the police, even though it took half an hour for her to die. I don't need a pee any more. Perhaps I'm getting dehydrated. Or perhaps the fluid has returned to the organs in my body that need it most. I think about the time Edward zipped me into a sleeping bag, upside down, before going off on a bicycle trip with his mates. Their aim was to stop me following them. I try to recall the sensation of lying shut in that sleeping bag, the lack of air, the feeling of being unable to move. I know I lay in there for several hours, but I don't remember how it felt to be released again.

Mum stood on the edge of the lawn, where there was still some sunshine, smoking, deep in conversation with Karin. They were both smiling, Karin was nodding and Mum was waving her arms. I walked across to them. Hi, Karin, I didn't see you in church, I said. We hugged. Karin said she'd arrived late and had had to squeeze in between two of the designer-label set. Unni's been telling me about her latest project at work, she said. About art and faith. Right, I said. You haven't said anything about it to me, Mum. Oh, haven't I? she said. It's such a broad subject. Oh? I said. What do you mean? Mum's gaze wandered towards the entrance of the chapel. So what do the two of you think then, about art and faith, Mum? She turned and looked at me. It's a question of devotion. Both art and faith require devotion. A surrendering to the pain of life. She spoke very slowly, as though searching for the exact words to express her thoughts. In what way? I asked. Pain, she said, is what enables growth. Karin nodded. And what exactly, I asked, is the meaning of this pain? Don't we grow when we're happy? Mum looked at me; she seemed angry and said nothing. She leant her head back, exhaled and stared into the sky. I turned to Karin. She was looking at a young woman. She had a shaved head like Karin's. Mum was looking at the chapel door again. It's a nondescript door, you have to know about it to find it, or be taken to it by somebody who knows the way. The pastor had just come out. He was talking to a little group, committee members, no doubt. He was dressed entirely in black, with a lightweight coat that went just over the knee and a long black scarf. Where was the little boy? Mum turned to me, looked at me seriously, she seemed to be searching my face for an answer. Her hand trembled slightly. She dropped her cigarette to the ground, nodded to herself and headed across the square. Shall we go for a coffee? asked Karin. Sure, I said, why not? I felt tired. What I really wanted was to go home to bed, to sleep through Sunday and fast-forward to Monday, to campus, to the canteen. Oh, Ivar. I can see his hand around a cup as he passes it to me, those large, oblong nails, every little joint, each perfectly formed knuckle. Shouldn't we wait for Unni? asked Karin. Mum had gone over to the pastor and we saw them greet one another. The three students said goodbye to him, he followed them momentarily with his eyes as they went off, presumably in the direction of Lorry, their favourite café. Mum was talking, waving one hand in the air, while the other rummaged in her handbag for a packet of cigarettes. We might be some time then, I said. I didn't want to call out to Mum with so many people about. Let's go, I said. We wouldn't have to stay long, Mum and I could still go to the cinema later. Karin and I headed towards Hegdehaugsveien. I looked down at the paving, at the withered leaves and grass. I think I felt a heavy sadness, and yet an unbelievable lightness, as though I were happy. I didn't know why. I looked up at the sky and the pale autumn sun. Everything was so intense, so real. A thought came to me. I'd finally found something to say that was unique to me. You know something, I said, I always find it strange to think about God when I look at nature. He seems somehow more present indoors, in a room, in a social space, rather than out in the fresh air, in the trees or the clouds. Karin didn't seem to understand. Or she didn't agree. My forehead, eyebrows and temples ached, the stress of my studies, no doubt, or my eternally bad conscience.

Footsteps through the park. The trees, the fresh air. I think of us, Ivar, you and me. We were leaning out of the window, it was cold, the middle of the night, we were naked and said nothing, you were smoking, and we looked east over the city, and at the illuminated sky. I wanted to tell you how my life had suddenly changed. Each time we planned to meet, I felt sure everything would disintegrate, vanish, be gone: that the momentum would cease and everything come to a standstill, leaving a vacuum. But here we were. Standing at the window together. And with each moment, a new and ever truer pattern emerged; in what we saw, and inside too. I wanted to tell you that, when you're with me, everything of beauty comes into focus. But you've gone now and I can't talk to you. Maybe you'll never come back. And now I'm crying again, Ivar. You'd have called me a cry-baby, wouldn't you? And you'd have kissed the tears from my cheeks, wouldn't you? And held me, Ivar, held me tight. Tight. You would, wouldn't you, Ivar? That's true, isn't it? Isn't it?

I stood in front of the hallway mirror. My hair hung around my face. I was trying to make it lie flat, so it wouldn't fall into my eyes without being tucked behind my ears. You should wear it up, Mum said. She'd come up behind me from the kitchen. We'd had eggs on toast for lunch, and I'd persuaded her to come and see *Betty Blue* with me. It was showing at Frogner Cinema again. You've got a flat back to your head, she said, so you should wear your hair up to balance it out. She demonstrated what she meant with her own hair. I watched her in the mirror, turning her head this way and that, gazing at her reflection. A girl on my course had told me in a lecture break that I should wear it loose. I'd taken my hairclip out and was putting it back in when she said I should leave my hair down. I'd never considered it before. I look like a nice, sensible girl with it pinned back. Pretty and sweet. You're so intelligent, Mum said suddenly, our eyes meeting in the mirror. It sounded as though the thought had never crossed her mind before, as though it took her by surprise. What do you mean? I said. Intelligent? She nodded to herself, frowning. I put my hairclip in as usual, tugging out a few strands around my ears, nineteenth-century costume drama style. I looked at myself. You're so strong and beautiful, Karin had said in the café. So wise and knowledgeable. I remember looking at her across the table. It was a nice thing to say. I smiled, but it didn't sink in, it seemed meaningless, an insult almost. A tram had passed the café window. I remember the face of a little girl on the tram. She was wearing a red woolly hat, and she'd placed her gloves between her cheek and the window. I remember thinking how desolate she looked, gazing out; perhaps she'd taken the tram alone, or hadn't pressed the bell when she should. Karin was saying something about our never discussing God, about it being too big and personal a subject. But that for her, as a pastor, it was vital to formulate things, even if they seemed unclear. I need to be able to talk about God with conviction, she said. I never know what to say when people go on about God like that. I feel guilty that I don't think about Him or Her more, but whenever I do, it just slips away from me. There's something in the idea that if we understood everything, God would cease to be bigger than us, and we would no longer need Him. It's an argument I fall back on; even if it doesn't really stand up, it helps momentarily. Forgive me, Father, show me the right path, and give me the strength to believe without doubt. We've got to go now, Mum, I said, turning away from the mirror. The seating isn't numbered. I'm not quite ready, she said. I'll be quick. She disappeared into the bathroom. I heard her sit on the toilet. Nothing was happening. Mum! I said. I stood there in that empty apartment. That's how I remember it, empty, even though we all lived here then, the entire family. It was the middle of the day and I'd sneaked back home from nursery, to tell Mum about a toy I really wanted, a plastic red bus conductor's bag, with multicoloured paper tickets. She walked into the lounge, a cigarette in her mouth. She looked so happy. But the instant she saw me, her face dropped. I don't remember what I said, just that I clambered back over the fence into the nursery garden and that nobody had noticed my absence. Mum, I said, are you coming? I heard her sigh, then a few drops of pee, toilet paper being pulled out, an excessively long strip. You use much too much loo roll, I said through the door. Mum? I open the bathroom door and she's lying on the floor, beaten unconscious, clumps of hair on the purple mat, black bruises on her neck, two oval shaped thumb marks. Mum opened the bathroom door with her trousers round her ankles. I was just thinking… she said. She took the plastic off a tampon while she talked. What? I said. She stuck the tampon in, still looking at me. Well, she said as she bent down to grab her panties and then pull her trousers up, the tight variety she favours. Well, I was thinking we could maybe write a card. Who to? I asked. She went over to the mirror and began to comb her hair thoughtfully. To your brother. To Edvard, she said. Sure, I said.

We walked arm in arm in the street under the autumn trees. Are you sure this movie's my kind of thing? said Mum. Yes, I said. It's French and it's a love film. And does it have a happy ending? Not exactly, but it's a good movie and worth seeing. Are you sure? Yes, Mum, and it's just a movie. You should at least give it a chance. I held the door open for her when we arrived at the cinema. Mum bought the tickets. She was paying. We exchanged glances as we walked past the confectionery counter and shook our heads in unison. No treats tonight. We entered the dark auditorium. I wanted to go to the front, Mum preferred to stay further back; we sat halfway, in the middle of a row. We ought to have been closer to the screen. I tried telling myself not to waste any more energy on it. You're sitting here now, Johanne, just relax, I thought. At least you're not in chains. I had to smile at my method of consoling myself. I thought about the opening scene of the movie. Karin told me she walked out, because they were at it so long. But after that there are all those beach huts they're going to paint. That's the best bit, with the best shots, I just love it, and I think that the tempestuous Betty, who flings everything out of the window and comes down the stairs with her suitcases, ready to leave – well, she's me.

She couldn't get enough air. Wasn't breathing into her stomach. She stood frozen, her mouth gaping, however hard she tried to close it. Her hand trembled as she struggled to light her cigarette. You are so unkind, she said. You knew that wasn't my kind of film. She started to walk on. Mum, I said, not moving. I didn't know what to say. She was never angry, never shouted, she was the kind of mum who understood and tolerated most things, the perfect pedagogue. It wasn't meant like that, I said. I thought you'd enjoy it, the beginning at least. She turned on me and screamed, The beginning! Do you have any idea, Johanne? Do you have any idea what love is? Have you any concept of what it can be? Sex is not the same as love. You can't just show off your breasts and think that that'll make men love you. She pouted and half closed her eyes. She was clearly poking fun at Betty, but it felt as if she was imitating me. That film portrays women in the most appalling way, she said. What does that girl have to contribute other than her body? She's nothing but a mirror for the man. And if that's what you think love is, then you're welcome to it, darling. That film knows nothing about women or women's sexuality. Nothing. She took several deep drags on her cigarette. People stared at us as they were leaving the cinema. I didn't know what to say. She was probably right. I should have realized it wasn't her kind of film. A love film! she said. That is sex, covert violence and rape. Murder, Mum said. And you knew it. You deceived me, tricked me into coming. You're not nice. Her voice seemed to stick to the walls, so its imprint would be permanent and I'd hear it whenever I walked past, Mum's voice screaming at me, echoing between the walls, like the noise of a helicopter scouring the terrain, nothing escaping its scrutiny. I can't accept your deceiving me, said Mum. I didn't think she'd ever been so angry. I put up with a lot of things, she said, you know I do, but this I will not tolerate. What do you mean? I said. She didn't reply. I thought about my plan, my finances, my future. Had I ruined it all by taking her to this movie? Perhaps I'd have to move out and get a student loan. Perhaps I'd never be able to afford an apartment. You mean The Barns won't happen? I asked. She said nothing, just stared at me. I don't know, she answered. Her voice was faint. Maybe, maybe not. I just can't stand any more manipulation, she said. I want things to be real between us. What do you mean real? I asked. We should be honest in everything we say to each other. I should be honest and you should be honest. God keeps our actions in his heart, Johanne. I'll never let anyone deceive me again. Not even you. She turned and started to walk away. Her back suddenly seemed round and stooped, her steps slow, and I felt so sorry for her. She looked so small and lonely. Mum! I yelled, but she didn't turn. I've never wanted to lie to you, I thought. I've only ever wanted to be kind. I do try to be nice, Mum. But maybe I hadn't been. Maybe I couldn't see myself from the outside. Maybe I was terrible. A despicable lump of nothing, wicked and manipulative. It was calculating of me to use her the way I did, living off her. My plan, my entire life was based on endless scheming, I'd even calculated on going to heaven when I died. You're sly and exploitative, Johanne. She's right, I thought, you're not nice. I followed her for a few steps and then stopped. She turned right at Frognerveien and I lost sight of her. And there I stood. It's true, Johanne, you're a pig. A pig that gorges on other people's food and money. But that's how she wants it. She wants me to live with her. She's the one who talks about The Barns. It was her idea. I was getting cold and started to walk. I had to face up to the fact that I had no valid defence. It was even true that I'd been unsure that she'd like the movie. My back ached. It was stiffer than ever. I tried to stretch it a bit as I walked, but it hurt even more.

I walked along the wide Frogner streets up to the market square. I took the steps that lead up to the children's playground and followed Professor Dahlsgate. I was freezing, despite walking. I reckoned, it probably served me right. I thought about the other students at university. Karin, for example, she lives in student digs at Kringsjå and gets by all right. They have a strength, a capacity for survival, that I don't possess. I'm different, not like them, I have something lacking, a flaw. I have a hole out of which all my strength seems to drain. There's no point comparing. Staying with Mum and then living at The Barns. That was my secret. My safety net. It ensured that this hole would go unnoticed, that I could manage as well as all the other girls. The Barns, two yellow-painted houses, one with a round window, the clematis and honeysuckle along the wall by the kitchen, the sun through the leaves in the large trees, the light coming in through the windows, making patterns on the floors. Quiet, peace, harmony. No more pressures, no loan instalments to pay. Without The Barns it'll be too difficult, I thought. I'll never manage it. Never. I remembered Watson and his psychology theory. His black box of the 1920s. The box represents the organism, us, but Watson wasn't interested in what happens inside us, since it is impossible to design an experiment to measure that with any degree of accuracy. To his mind it was more important to investigate the stimulus that gave the adequate and desired response. This, he felt, would be measurable and useful. I crossed Josefinesgate and headed towards Bislett. I tried to think of myself as a black box. And Mum too. I had to find the stimulus Mum needed. A soft, gentle voice and a big hug. Reassurance. I thought about the sheets of paper covered with sketches, designs I've made of The Barns. They hang on the wall in the hall. They are luminous at night, shining at me as I head to the toilet. I'm sitting with my back against the door now, remembering that night and how I wished I could be a structural or architectural drawing on a huge

piece of transparent paper. Then we could each spread
our sheets on top of each other, Mum and I, and see
where our lines diverged. And we could take an eraser
and adjust them to match.

I started the walk up Bergstien. The street lamps threw
delicate yellow rings onto the asphalt and up the walls. I
turned the corner and looked over at the church. It was
lit up. A holy meeting place. Why wasn't I frightened?
I'd have been terrified now. After all, it's right next to the
huge cemetery where so many things happen at night. But
casting my mind back, all I remember is that I smiled, even
though my back ached and Mum had been angry. I was
happy. Or, to be more precise, there was a separate space
inside me for Ivar. And at that moment that was where
I was. In that good space, I was happy. It started to rain,
just a few drops, and I stood under the big trees, smiling.
I was here again. I wondered if the church was open and
if it was possible to go in. I went through the gate and up
to the door. It was locked. Coming back through the gate,
I saw a notice on the bulletin board outside the railings
stating that the church was open daily from ten until twelve.
I turned. Now was the moment, I thought, that he should
walk past. Now that I was alone. If I'd known Ivar's full
name, I thought to myself, I could have looked him up in
the phone book and found his exact address. What was it
Mum always said? Shattered dreams. No, Ivar was good.
I wanted to touch that bushy brown hair and kiss him,
the freckles, the gentle smile. There was no need for us
to sleep together, we could get to know each other first,

establish our relationship. Sex is overrated, I thought, we pay it far too much attention. Love is what's important. I imagined myself in Ivar's apartment, looking out of his window one night, gazing down here at the church and at the girl waiting under the trees near the gate. And she would no longer be alone. I headed for home, listening as I walked for footsteps to come running after me, a breathless man with freckles and rain on his face. I started to worry at how wide awake I felt. You'll lie in bed unable to sleep, and tomorrow you'll get no coursework done, you'll be nodding off all the time. What are you doing here, Johanne? Why are you deluding yourself? What in heaven's name are you thinking of?

I try to open my mouth, but it's as though my tongue has swollen up, grown too big. It's like having a reverse cock in my mouth, a large swollen penis attached inside me. I close my eyes, and when I open them, it's gone. It must have been a dream. I'm very thirsty and need to pee again; this time I empty the rubbish bin in the corner behind the door and crouch down.

I turned the key. I had to deal with the alarm before I let myself in: there's a small key that activates the switch, after which I have ten seconds to get in, close the door and turn the handle from inside. Fortunately we've never had any need of it. The ceiling light was on in the hall. I turned it off. I hate the harsh light from above, bleaching the life out of everything and casting ugly shadows. I couldn't see if Mum had switched the light off behind her curtain. I took my jacket off. I had to go into the kitchen to put my foot up on the bench, so I could undo my laces. I went into the lounge and knocked on the wall next to the curtain. A moment passed. Then there was a yes. She sounded tired. Probably still upset over the movie incident. I was desperately hoping that everything would be all right.

Dearest, sweetest Mum. I pulled the curtain aside. She was propped up on her pillows in her nightdress, reading. She didn't look up from her book. Why do I always try to impose change on her, force things on her that she doesn't like? I should never have taken her. I had no idea how I'd manage without her. Nobody would suspect it, because from the outside I seem to have everything going for me: hard-working, bright, a good conversationalist, with long, curly red hair that people compliment me on. What obstacle could there be to success? When one is clever and reasonably pretty? I felt it coming, but I didn't want Mum to see me cry. She'd started a new novel. She must have finished the Swedish book. I couldn't see the title of this one. She went on reading. I moved closer to her bed. I didn't know what to do – perhaps I should sit down, but her bed is so high, she has bookshelves under it on the sides that aren't against a wall. She finally looked up, peering at me over her glasses with raised eyebrows. Well? she said. Are you still cross with me? I asked. She looked down at her book again. Yes, she said, although she sounded sad more than anything. Sad and tired. I went to see Mother after the service today, after you disappeared so suddenly, she said. I was hoping we'd go together, you know how draining I find it when I go up there. Yes, I said. She isn't well, said Mum. What do you mean? I said. Those new drugs still make her dizzy, and I suggested she ought to get a personal alarm, said Mum. Yes, I said, that sounds sensible. For my sake, Mum said. She could do it for my sake. I live in constant fear that she'll end up lying there. Oh, I can't bear the thought, she said. I imagined Granny, her rotund body, stretched on the floor. Shall I talk to her? I said. Mum fixed her eyes on me seriously, without answering. She looked very tired. If you could, she said slowly, that would be wonderful. Of course I can, I said. Oh, thank you so much, said Mum. She took off her reading glasses to wipe her eyes – they tend to run whenever she's lying down – she used the sleeve of her nightie, leaving black streaks from the make-up she hadn't washed off. I can go straight from uni tomorrow, I said. I'll cycle up. You're an angel, she said, smiling wearily. I don't know what I'd do without you.

I lay on my bed staring up at the ceiling, trying to breathe deeply into my stomach, hoping to loosen up my stiff back. I imagined the surface of a cheek that had been slashed with a knife, flesh oozing, like when you slit the belly of a fish. I thought about Martha and Mary. Mary sat at Jesus's feet and listened while Martha prepared the food. It's easy to nod at this story and assume that it's Mary who does the right thing by listening to the word of the Lord, dropping her tasks and coming to Him. But I couldn't stop thinking about Martha, what it must have been like to be her. Was her work without value? Her expression of devotion through that meal, her concrete, physical care: did that, I wondered, count for nothing? I would stand in the doorway of that stone house, full of shadows, and I would say, Hello, Martha, that bread smells wonderful. Yes please, I'd love a little soup. We would sit at the long table. Martha would smile shyly. I'd tell her how lovely she was; I'd have to ask Karin to teach me how to say that in Hebrew. And we'd leave Jesus and Mary sitting there. As I drifted off to sleep, I stood looking out of the round window of my cottage. There was sand everywhere. The house was standing on the ocean floor. There was water outside the window. People were coming on horseback. I could hear them in the distance. Or was it a helicopter? I hid on the top shelf of my wardrobe. I curled up and hoped they'd never find me.

The sun slants in through the bars of the window, waking her up. Her left ankle has swollen around the chain. She finds the patch of pillow where the sunlight touches her whole face. She closes her eyes, trying not to think of what lies ahead of her today. It won't be long before the sun gets too hot. I glanced over at the dazzling light on the wall opposite, across the backyard. So harsh it stung my newly woken eyes, bringing tears to them. It was Monday morning, six thirty. At seven thirty, I usually cycle from home. I had to get up. I tried to sit, but was prevented by my stiff back. I was forced to lie on my side, roll onto my stomach and throw my legs out, so as to climb down. Standing in the shower, I thought about what I'd been dreaming when I woke up. I had the keys to a pharmaceuticals factory. It was night and I'd let myself in and was walking through long corridors that reminded me of a school. I opened the stock cupboard and stole little see-through bags of pills, Rohypnol, Valium and morphine. At one point a crowd of men in suits emerged from a meeting and nearly caught me. I hid behind a door. I tried to work out what the dream meant.

I've never messed about with any drugs or medications. We barely take a single pill in our house, everything is psychological: if you're ill it's because you're not getting all the love and attention you need. I was almost always healthy as a child, but Edvard was so ill several times that he had to be taken to hospital in an ambulance. Perhaps I was receiving the attention that was rightly his. I heard Mum in the kitchen, putting the coffee on. I turned the shower off. I shouldn't linger. My schedule in the mornings is tight, there's no time to get lost in thought. I had to focus on what needed doing, on making more coffee for my Thermos, packing my sandwiches, eating a quick breakfast, and on the best order to do things; whether it was most efficient to put the coffee on before making my packed lunch and eating. Mum was sitting in the lounge, with the newspaper spread out on the coffee table. Hello, I said. No answer. I stopped in the doorway. Mum, I said. I waited for her to turn towards me. If I'm going to see Granny, I won't be back in time for dinner. She went on reading. Take the money that's in my purse, she said, so you can get lunch in the canteen. OK, I said. Thanks.

Cycling up towards Majorstua, I was struck by the colours of the trees. Thank you, Father, for these fresh, clear autumn days. The world is infinitely beautiful and bountiful. I knew that I'd almost certainly see Ivar soon. And that, I thought, is enough. Just to see him, take him in, take things step by step, gently, carefully. My fingers were frozen. Maybe I should spend that fifty-kroner note on some gloves. But it was jumble sale season, so

I could go next Saturday and buy a pair for a couple of kroner, maybe even leather ones. I thought of all the things I could buy with fifty kroner. Or perhaps I could put it in the account where I'm saving money for my own apartment, if nothing comes of The Barns. I could start eating less too and put the money I'd have spent on food into that account too. I do all our shopping with Mum's card, she'd never notice, it would roughly add up to the same amount. I thought about how much an apartment would actually cost. You'll never make it, Johanne. I tried to put my back into pedalling uphill, but it was still stiff. Amazing I could cycle at all.

I'm imagining Ivar on the plane. I have just an image of his body reclining in his seat, there's no sound, no colour, he doesn't speak to me, doesn't see me looking at him, or that I'm sitting beside him. I should have been sitting next to him and we should have been leaning towards the window, watching the clouds. He had bought a double set of earphones for his Walkman so we could listen to music on the journey together. I can hear the joy in his voice when he showed them to me, look Johanne, look. Maybe he's putting it on now, leaning his head back, closing his eyes, listening. He smiles at the stewardess as she comes with food and coffee. He seems so happy there on his own. Maybe he doesn't miss me at all. Maybe he's relieved to have escaped me. He is free now.

It's dark by the entrance to the reading rooms. I don't know if it's the low ceiling or there's just too little light. I stood by the banisters at the bottom of the stairs trying to look relaxed, despite being so hot from cycling uphill. I recognized most of the people there, they usually arrived at opening time too, preferably a minute or two before. The guy in the red-checked shirt came up the stairs, blue cycle helmet in one hand and nylon bag over his shoulder, ash-blond hair standing on end. He regularly walks straight past us to the reading room, jumping the queue, then presses his forehead against the locked doors, a gesture of salutation, or receiving some sort of blessing, or forgiveness perhaps, before leaning his back against them with a sigh. He always arrives at the last minute, sweating and out of breath, just before the man with the keys comes to open up and the rest of us who were hanging about on the landing amble in and claim our places. Not that they're ours, of course, but it's as if we commandeer them, reigning over the reading room until nine o'clock. Which is when the others come. I try not to think of their lives. Late nights, friends, studio flats, loud music. A shared house perhaps.

Walking into the kitchen. Meeting a familiar face. Laughing, talking, putting the kettle on. Lovers' tiffs and the slamming of doors. Taking the days as they come, with no particular plan. And the worst is that they manage for themselves. They drift about and things turn out fine. I know I'm not like that. I have to struggle for what they take for granted. I have to play it safe. Have to stay on track, every day. It's the little steps that count, straight ahead. Reading all the chapters on the reading list meticulously. Every day. Anything else would result in stepping off course, which would lead to another little step, and another, and another. I'd lose my balance completely and never get to be a psychologist. What they display, these students who don't arrive in the reading room until nine, or even later, is a kind of daring. They play with life, with possibilities. For me my studies are like a tightrope I'm balancing on, life will begin only when I've reached the other side. Only when I'm standing there triumphantly, with a glowing testimonial and glittering results, only then, I think to myself, will I be free. You're going over old ground now, Johanne. That's the way I am. I have written it down in my blue notebooks hundreds of times. Mum says she has a deep respect for other people's privacy and that she'd never look, for example, through the blue hard-backed Chinese books I fill with my notes. A voice lives between their pages, my very own conversation partner, a being that has no independent existence, but which emerges in what I write, in the way I write. A voice that really cares about me, that listens.

I sat in the reading room and took out my developmental psychology book: confusing and impossible to grasp. Piaget is boring. I agree with his central theses about assimilation and accommodation, the notion of conservation of weight, that we strive for balance in our learning, and that we have a hunger, an inner authority that drives us on. But I don't like the stages he sets out, his schematic approach, his boxes. Which is why I hate Piaget. I'd spit on him if I could, for what he does to life. Outlining it, cutting it up. I realized I hadn't turned on the little lamp over my desk. When I pressed the switch the book was suddenly bathed in a new light, pleasant and warm. I tried to breathe into my stomach. I sat up straight and looked out over the empty desks. Screwing my eyes up, the whole room became a yellowish haze. A hot sandy beach. There was a rattling noise, moving along the aisles that divide the reading room. Someone was collecting cups and cutlery to take back to the canteen. The trolley was clearly made of steel, I could hear every object as it was put down. I sat listening. I looked towards the aisle, waiting for somebody to appear between the partitions. The white jacket, the brown bushy hair. Yes! It was him. Ivar. My gaze met his. It was as though he could see I'd been thinking about him all weekend. I bent over my book and looked at the picture, a child wearing nothing but a nappy and sandals, walking along a road near some parked cars and pulling a toy duck after it on a string. Above it, the title Sleeping and Waking. You got any cups here? he said behind me. I hadn't heard his footsteps on the thin carpet. He poked his head round the pillar as he looked at me, and smiled. I shook my head and felt myself blush. He stood there for a moment, and we looked at each other in silence. Then he smiled again and moved on. He seemed so calm, as though he had endless amounts of time. And he does, I thought, not being a student. He didn't stop at anyone else's desk. I smiled. I looked at the clock; there was still another hour before my first lecture. I suddenly felt hot. I had to remove the jumper that I always drape over my shoulders when I work. I heard the trolley go down the central aisle and through the swing doors, followed by a bumping noise as it went over the threshold of the main door, then nothing. I bent back over my book. The next chapter was about the brain. There was a diagram showing the nerve development in a baby's cortex from birth up to two years. It looked like a forest, its branches sparse at first, then growing denser, a mass of twigs going in all directions. I thought about the garden at The Barns. It would be my responsibility. I pictured the apple trees, pear blossom, leaves, his face, the sun shining, Ivar walking towards me across the lawn. I'd borrow gardening books from the library when I'd finished my exams. I adore climbing plants and hanging ones too, we'll have a Virginia creeper on the main house, it's a classic, it'll be so beautiful. Turning up, disrupting my concentration like that! I couldn't read now. Every word in the book had become a new code for his name. I had a rectangular patch from my breastbone to my navel without skin, it stung. He should have considered that. His eyes gave the impression of having so much compassion for the world. And yet he went around messing everything up. I tried to read on: There are three main temperament types. Researchers agree that the temperament is innate to the personality; the rest is more or less dependent, they think, on environment. There are three categories of baby: easy, difficult and slow to warm up. Slow infants tend to have a low activity level, they appear sleepy, adapt slowly, don't engage to begin with, and tend not to be as good-humoured as the easy child. The child's temperament should match the mother's. If the mother is quick and impatient, the slow child risks not having time to warm up before she gives up, causing the child to be understimulated. These three temperament types are illustrated with drawings showing infants at mealtimes. Each drawing shows a child sitting in a highchair wearing a bib. A hand is feeding it with a spoon. The easy baby beams, with the spoon in its mouth. The difficult child waves its arms, food spills out of an overturned bowl, the child has gone red in the face and its mouth is wide open, screaming. The slow child has its head turned away. I remember Mum saying that I smiled a lot as a baby. Perhaps it's true. I imagined Mum turning her head. Her hair swung in front of her face. I caught a glimpse of her eyes. No longer blue, but grey. I tried to picture myself opening my mouth. I couldn't. I saw the girl lying strapped to a bed. The sun shone. There was sweat on her breasts, in her groin. A man was standing in the doorway, skinny, long red hair and wearing an earring. Something was wrong. I didn't know what.

I suddenly pushed my chair back and rose to my feet. I had to smile, I'd done it without thought, unpremeditatedly, without weighing the pros and cons. I just stood up. Perhaps I should take it seriously, I thought, this body of mine. If it refused to sit still, it must be after something. I knew I had a few coins in my pocket. I left the reading room, went down the stairs and stopped at the entrance to the canteen. I looked in. Seating areas, partitions, plants. I didn't feel I had the strength. Father, I prayed, I know you are everywhere, even here. I remembered an old film I'd seen on TV as a child, about Greek gods, the figures ran from place to place on tracks, their mechanisms clanking and scraping. It had terrified me. I tried to imagine I was one of those figures on a track and that what I was about to do would propel me forward. Johanne, you're only getting a coffee. There were one or two people sitting by the window. Further away near the counter was a table of five girls. Their voices dominated the room. They talked in turns, bursting into intermittent laughter.

Hello there. His voice sounded happy, almost surprised. We stood there with the counter between us. And when he looked at me, I felt the contours of my body, as though I was encircled by flames. I'll just have a coffee, I said. Five minutes? he asked. He didn't take his eyes off me and we stood perfectly still. I wanted to say something but felt my mouth drop open. Why, I didn't know. I'll be right back, he said. I bit my lip, frowned, pulled myself together, put a cup under the machine, pressed the button, let the coffee run, took it over to the till and paid. The start of my financial ruin, spending my money in the canteen, I thought. He came out of the swing doors near the washing-up with a mug in his hand and a packet of tobacco. Behind me the girls laughed again. I walked over to him. We headed for the exit where we'd first met. What are you studying? he asked. Psychology, I said. I knew that, of course, he said, smiling and looking straight at me. He'd got my phone number from the student council. I felt myself blush. It was lovely to see you there, in the street, on Friday, he said. I've been thinking about you, imagining you, he said. I wandered the streets hoping I'd bump into you again. His words made me feel light. Happy. Do you live nearby? he asked. So he hadn't checked my address. Or perhaps Mum had given him the impression there was no Johanne living there, since he'd rung so late. I told him I lived in Frogner and asked if he'd worked in the canteen for long. He'd only been there since the beginning of term. I knew that, of course. I'd have noticed him, I thought to myself. He played the guitar, had a band, and spent all his time making music. The job was just a way of earning money, something to live on. We went outside and stood next to the wall. He dug out a ready-made rollie from the bottom of the packet, put it between his lips and lit up. I watched his mouth close softly around the cigarette, somehow gentle and good; he seemed so honest as he inhaled, his cheeks hollowed, he looked incredibly thin. Was he a bit wimpish perhaps? There was something sad about his eyes, they were so pale, almost colourless, as though someone had sliced off a layer. Maybe he's lonely, I thought. I wanted to take care of him, stroke his hair, give him proper food. We're doing a gig tonight, a basement party, a surprise for some students at the Academy, something the guys from the architecture department thought up, he said. Want to come? I didn't know what to say. It was so unexpected, too sudden. What I wanted most was to go for a walk in the forest, just the two of us, talking, alone, with the sun coming through the trees at an angle, looking at it together, getting to know each other. Ivar took a folded piece of yellow paper out of his pocket. Here's the address and time and stuff, he said. He looked at me with his head to one side. He was serious. His lips moved a fraction, I observed the breath between them, and his freckles. He'll kiss me now, I thought. My lips were tingling, but nothing happened. He just looked at me, his face very close. It was as if we'd made a promise to each other, exchanged a vow that had no outward expression, because it was unvoiced, but it would live on inside me for ever, real and genuine. Pure. I think Ivar felt it too. Like the words I love you. But then why, I wondered, hadn't he kissed me? Did he think I was ugly? Repulsive? What was he after? A basement party somewhere near the Akerselva river, late at night. What did he intend to subject me to? Why me? Men always accost me when I'm in town or on the train, alcoholic kids, guys who are out of their heads, or who need someone to confide in. There must be something about me, something they see. Perhaps I'm marked. Perhaps I have a wound that everybody can see but me. Something wrong? Ivar asked, putting a hand on my arm. I still hadn't answered him about the party. His grasp was firm. A strong, warm hand on my arm. That's how it starts. So-called concern, I thought later. Just another word for manipulation. But he's so handsome. He seems so kind. Why couldn't he just have kissed me? I looked at my watch and told him I had to get back to my books. He nodded, said something about extended coffee breaks early in the day. We smiled at each other in the hall and he took my empty cup. See you tonight then, he called after me, as I went down the spiral staircase to the toilets. I sat in the big disabled cubicle. I noticed I was swollen when I wiped myself, slightly tingly and prickly. I wondered if I had an infection. Some sort of fungus. I pictured Ivar's eyes like two tiny micro-organisms swimming around beneath the skin of my vulva.

Good God. The words slipped out of me as I was walking down the footpath towards the Sophus Lie auditorium. Good God, Johanne. I said the Lord's Prayer several times over. A chain reaction. My nipples were hard, almost rigid. Cognitive psychology. Visual agnosia. You can see but are unable to attach any meaning to what you see, or you interpret it incorrectly. Or when you finally manage to connect the visual information to the corresponding category or concept in your brain, it has taken so long that it becomes impossible for you to function normally. I looked down at my notepad. A4 unlined. Preferably bleached, white. I couldn't write any proper notes, the desk was too low and my back was too stiff. The lecturer was gripping the chalk between three fingers, his little finger sticking out stiffly. I doubted he knew how it made him look. I could never love a man who held his finger out like that, I thought. Would Ivar hold chalk like that? We must determine whether the damage is organic. The student representative arrived late and sat down next to me. She started rustling about in her handbag. A plastic bag. The zip on her pencil case. Finally she took out the electrical stimulator she always holds against her temple. Something must have happened when she was a child, a blow to the head, damaging the sensitivity to certain impulses and slowing the neurotransmitters. I was sleepy, cognitive psychology bores me, it's devoid of any magic. Still, I know it's important to understand it for the future, when I open my practice.

At break she wanted to discuss shelf space and reading-room places. I said that I needed the toilet, a lie. Father, forgive me. I went up the stairs, through the hall and out into the courtyard. Why did she have to sit next to me? Her stimulator gave off a hum. It disturbed me. I wouldn't be able to take much in during the next lecture, the noise would irritate me, and then I'd get a headache halfway through from trying to remember what had been said. Nobody knows what all this costs me. I mustn't lose my grip. But now I felt it coming over me, the tears welling up. Like a pathetic little puppy whining inside me. I forced them back and walked into the auditorium.

The lecturer was discussing one of the case studies on our curriculum. The patient has a tiny blood clot somewhere in the rear cortex that affects his perception, so that it takes him a long time and a huge amount of energy to register and respond to stimulae. It says somewhere in the textbook that his wife gives him medication. But what medication? The explanations in this book leave so many questions unanswered. Lecturers make it all so simple. That's probably the main reason for following lectures closely: things that present such knotty problems on the page make sense when the teacher talks, are unravelled, smoothed out. I looked around at my future colleagues. Everybody was bent over their notes. To the left, just below me, two mature women sat side by side. Bolt upright in their seats, they each had a notepad in their lap on a rigid board. Their make-up was flawless. They were dressed tastefully in muted colours, discreet, with expensive handbags and proper fountain pens. They were on the second row, at eye level with the lecturer. Whenever he said something funny they smiled, never quite breaking into a laugh. I wondered who in this room I would go to if I had problems. Anyone my own age looked silly, immature, unfocused. The older ones seemed too perfect and uptight. I couldn't find anyone I'd confide in. The only person I trusted here in this group, apart from God, was myself.

I didn't see any more of Ivar that day at Blindern. I didn't go into the cafeteria during lunch break. Not to buy another coffee. Or to see him. I remember thinking he hadn't kissed me. That was proof he'd only been kidding. He despised me. He hadn't even wanted to touch me, although the chance had been obvious enough. I decided I shouldn't ask him for anything. I would never go to him needing anything. I'd manage on my own. And now it's too late. I couldn't get to the airport on time even if a helicopter took me. Unless there's a delay, of course. Maybe I should shout out of the window and get someone to call the airport and find out if the departure for New York is delayed. Just imagine if the plane still hasn't taken off. I run to the exit and there's Ivar waiting for me, holding his arms out, reaching out to help me with my luggage. Useless fantasies, Johanne. Stick to reality. To the things you can do something about. Love yourself. The only thing I really know, the only thing I can trust, is my own strength, my own capacity for work. My body is muscular enough, it will carry me through, I am my own slave. Maybe I should spend this time in my room doing some exercise, so it's not completely wasted. I put my duvet on the floor and wedge my feet under the third step of my loft bed. I'll see how many sit-ups I manage. A hundred to each side is a minimum.

I remember cycling to Ullevål School later. It seems like another life now, going along those quiet roads towards Sagene. Tears ran down my cheeks in hot streaks. It struck me that my eyes probably looked beautiful at this moment, large, glossy. But God is the only one who sees me, I thought. God loves me, at least. That is my one blessing: God's love. I prayed as I whizzed downhill, before the long trek up to Tåsen. Be with me, Lord. Forgive me. The villas up there made me think of The Barns. It felt so good to think about that – a peaceful place in my head, a mental garden. I imagined seeing myself through the round window, walking around in my room, reading through papers, talking on the phone, waving my arms animatedly, so slender. I was wise, and actually rather beautiful and happy.

It would be five o'clock soon. I knew that Granny usually dozed off at about this time, or perhaps she'd already had her nap. I followed the busy main road up to her gate and then, standing with my bike between my legs, I peered into her mailbox. A few adverts and a community newsletter. Taking them, I pushed the gate open and wheeled my bike along the path. I looked up at the window; if she was awake she'd be sitting there. The red lamp was on. I couldn't see anyone inside. I propped my bike by the front steps, locked it, went up to the door and rang the bell, before going back down into the garden, so she could see me from her window on the second floor. She didn't know I was coming. I hadn't phoned to tell her. Nothing happened and I wondered if she'd heard the doorbell. I looked across at the traffic, at the cars whizzing past, motorcycles, a lorry. There were apples all over the lawn. I hadn't visited since the start of term. Everything seemed so small today: the house, the lawn, the garden. Whenever I thought of Granny's house and its surrounding garden, it was always enormous, the trees seemed bigger and taller. The walk from the house to the lawn, where I would have my home one day, seemed so long. Suddenly I thought that The Barns would never be a reality. They were already lost to me.

Hello, said Granny, so it's you. She'd opened the door a crack and poked her head round. She smiled mischievously as though I was an unannounced and longed-for suitor. Hello, I said, walking up the front steps, as she stepped back unsteadily to swing the door open and let me in. I leant forward to give her a hug; she recoiled slightly. Mum always says Grandad was very authoritarian. I've asked her what she means by that, whether perhaps he hit her, but I've never had an answer. I noticed that Granny had put on make-up. Streaks of foundation on her cheeks, a smudgy black on her eyebrows, mascara on her lashes and a fresh coat of bright pink on her lips matching her fingernails, and her thin cotton trousers and the little blouse under her white sweater. You're looking very smart, I said. Thank you, she said, touching her hair. She seemed happy.

I poured the coffee out for us. I had searched the cupboard for clean cups, while Granny had looked for the biscuits. I took the milk out of the fridge, poured her a drop, then put it back. She placed a sugar lump in her mouth and sipped her coffee through it. I ought to be stick thin, she said, eating as little as I do. She looked out of the window. I gazed round at all her things: the pink kitchen cabinets with gold handles, the plastic flowers in the vase on the side, the chequered linoleum floor. Mum wanted me to talk to you, I said. The muscles in her jaw tightened. She turned back towards the room and looked at me with her large, clear eyes, before raising her forefinger. Look out there, she said, turning back towards the window slowly and peering over her glasses. My eyes followed to where she was pointing. Further up the road were three Moelven Barracks in a row. Men are living there, you see. Yes, I said. And they walk around outside here, said Granny. I've never seen them come onto my property, but they walk around out there. And I don't like it. It's always been so quiet here, she said. But Granny, I said, they're working on the new roads. Girls come, she continued. I see them there, you know, in the middle of the day. Foreign girls. And the men go in to them. That leads to things, you know, Johanne. And in a nice district like this. She peered at me steadily over her glasses. I got up to fetch more coffee, she didn't want more, her cup was still almost full. I sat down again. Granny, I said, Mum wants you to… She interrupted. Your mother got in such a temper with me yesterday. It wasn't nice. But she has a demanding job and such an awful lot to do, so we'll let it pass. Now then, let's you and I enjoy ourselves, Johanne. She looked at me and smiled. She took a biscuit shaped like a little bow with a red blob in the middle, she pushed it gingerly between her teeth, lifted her lips and bit. She put the rest of the biscuit on her plate and lifted her cup with two fingers. I watched as the beige-coloured coffee met her pink lips. Then she pressed her left index finger to the corners of her mouth several times to remove the crumbs, although there were none there.

She followed me down the stairs when I left. She took one step at a time, holding the banister tightly as she went. When she reached the bottom she gripped the post with both hands and stared down into the carpet, her back stooped. I stood beside her, my foot lifted high on a stair to tie my laces. I tried to think what this stiff back meant, why it wasn't getting better, what it was telling me. Give me a ring then, I said. It's always nice to get a call. She was breathing fast and seemed paler than usual. She should take more exercise, if she went up and down the stairs more often she'd be in better shape. Bye then, Granny, I said, turning the latch and opening the door. It had got colder, a gust of wind blew in. I noticed Granny lift her shoulders as if to shield her ears. I knew I was going to freeze on my way home. Be careful, Johanne, she shouted after me. She watched me through the curtain at the door as I unlocked my bike and then as I rolled past she raised her hand and waved a couple of times before turning the security lock. It clicked twice and I imagined the rattle of the safety chain as she put it on.

I thought how much colder the evenings were turning. The sun was low and looked so red and warm when you were inside, but as I cycled off the wind blew down my collar and onto my chest and my nipples. Down at Sagene I saw two drunks in the park. They were standing there yelling into each other's faces. Granny had told me people rang on her doorbell at night, she'd go to the window and look, but they'd be gone, and then she'd lie half awake for the rest of the night, listening. Mum was trying to persuade her to install a burglar alarm, like the one we have at home. I can't remember when we got it, whether it was after that incident Mum had told me about, when a man had threatened her – she thought he had a shotgun hidden under his coat – or if it was later. It reminded me of attribution theory: your level of fear, or lack of it, is dependent on how you interpret the situation. An experiment was done in the 1950s designed to substantiate the notion that our feelings are guided by thoughts; that we think before we feel, that we are steered by our thoughts. It was linked to the age of optimism; the more we are controlled by thought, the more we can will ourselves to change. This is the driving force behind modern psychology, which is based on the indoctrination of the self. Through thought I can convince myself that the world is better than how I experience it; my pain will disappear, cease to exist, because I think differently. Just like this cold wind blowing through my clothes, I thought, as I freewheeled down Theresesgate, taking care to avoid the tram tracks, the cars parked either side, the traffic driving past. All I had to do was think that the wind was warm and I wouldn't notice the cold.

Yes, but Johanne dear, said Mum, a party on a Monday night? You've only just got home. I'd told her that Ivar had asked me. I'd decided to go. Maybe the fast cycle ride home and the wind had blown any self-destructive thoughts out of my head. Anyway. I'd picked out what I was going to wear. I was looking forward to seeing him again. Even if it would be from a distance, I wanted to see him; to watch him play, his guitar against his hips, his hands moving across the strings, the way he held it, his neck, his lips, his freckles. I'd show him I was tougher than he thought. That I wasn't to be messed with. I dared. I wanted. I would go. It wasn't as if I was asking him for anything. On the contrary, it was by *not* going that I'd be a bother. That would demand more on his side, feats of persuasion. By going, I'd be carrying my own weight; taking responsibility for myself. Mum sat at the kitchen table. I'd bought fresh unshelled prawns for us to have with French bread and mayonnaise, a taste of summer in this cold windy weather. They were on special offer at the ICA supermarket down in Theresesgate, I'd seen the offer as I cycled past. I'd made a salad too, baby spinach and mushrooms with a lemon dressing. I wanted to make Mum happy by preparing a special meal. I filled a jug with water and I turned to her with it in my hands. I could see prawn juice all around her mouth and on one cheek. She was wearing the tight trousers she always wears for work and a pretty, almost see-through top of woven linen, showing her bra, the delicate lace one, underneath. She seemed tired. It should have occurred to me that it might be irritating to have to bother to peel prawns when your stomach is rumbling with hunger. I suddenly remembered a time when I'd found her with a man; the loud groans, the creaking. I'd assumed they were having sex and I couldn't resist peeping between the gap in the curtain. He was on his knees by the bed rubbing pressure points under her foot. She had all her clothes on except her socks. Half an hour later he was gone. I imagined the sun coming in stripes through the barred window over the girl in her bed. I leant back against the wall to avoid the glaring lamplight. When Mum said the word party in that tone, it was as though she'd said sex. Sex on a Monday, Johanne? Yes, but Mum, I said, I don't have to stay late. You know I'm always careful about time. That I like to get enough sleep when I have to attend lectures the next day. Besides, I don't think Ivar's that much of a party type, he's working tonight, playing with his band. But I don't really know him yet, I thought. Perhaps she's right and I've got him completely wrong. I was lost for words. I cleared the table, rinsed the plates, told her she should leave the washing-up, I'd do it the next day. She didn't answer. Johanne, she said, there's been something about you these last few days. Is your period coming? A moment's silence. And then: You just seem a bit strange. You're not taking anything, are you? Silence again. There's an artist we've met through a seminar, he's working as a consultant on a project with us, and he said he... She hesitated. What are you getting at? I said. He told us he takes something, she said, when he's working. I turned and looked at her. I thought of my dream about the pharmaceuticals factory. Perhaps I'm repressing things, perhaps I'm not always conscious of what I'm doing. But Johanne, I thought, you know that's nonsense. You're a proper girl, you're a Christian, I thought with a smile. God is your happy pill. Mum gazed out of the window, doubtless thinking about this situation at work. She thinks a lot about work. Granny was right, it is a demanding job. She's head of department. Don't worry, I said. I went into my room and sat in the big chair. I leant my head back, trying to relax. My back was so stiff again, I couldn't bend it at all. I closed my eyes and prayed.

I've no idea how long I sat there in that chair. I'd normally be going to bed now. But I knew I should be getting ready to leave. I didn't move. Perhaps he's just leading me on, I thought. Then the door to my room opened. Mum stood in the doorway. She looked so sad. I think you ought to treat me properly, she said. Now she was talking she just seemed angry. I looked at her. I want you to communicate with me. I'm an adult, an intelligent person, she said. I'm so concerned about you, and I've got

Mother to worry about too. You should listen to me, not just go flitting off to parties. She stopped to draw breath. For heaven's sake, Johanne, she said. She looked at me, and lifting her left hand as if she'd gathered everything in her palm, she held it out for me to see, before waving it away. Then she stood there, as though expecting a reply. She put a cigarette in her mouth and took it out again without lighting it. She was wearing a new dress, short, black and tight, low-cut to reveal her delicate neckline. In one hand she had a long viscose leopard-patterned scarf. Had she knotted it around her wrist? Mum, I said gently. Dear, sweet, lovely Mum. I didn't know what more to say. She turned and went, leaving my door wide open, and I heard her pushing her curtain brusquely aside, signalling that I should follow her to continue the conversation. It was my turn now. I looked at my watch. It was already well past nine. I focused my thoughts on the party, clothes, money, on the possible cost, whether you had to pay to get in, how I'd get there and back. It hit me that I was going to see Ivar again soon. Like a punch of joy. I'd forgotten momentarily and now suddenly I remembered. I noticed myself smile. I was holding things too hard, my comb, my buttons, too hard and yet too loose. Was I shaking? I rushed into the shower, dried myself and slapped on a bit of make-up, shook my hair, it would have to stay loose. I found my dress and the fifty-kroner note I'd decided to put aside. I set it as a limit for myself. Fifty kroner, no more, OK? I chose shoes without laces so as not to have to bend over. My head seemed a white blank. Be with me,

O Lord, I thought. Slutty little Johanne. Dear, oh dear. I should go in there now and talk to her, battle it out, but it seemed impossible to talk to her *and* go to a party. It didn't feel as though the choice lay with me, rather it lay elsewhere, in the rush of the moment, in my body that moved of its own accord. I grabbed my keys, yelled out a conciliatory goodbye, opened the front door, set the alarm and left.

Fortunately, it wasn't raining. But the wind was still cold. I stopped my bicycle under a street lamp near Riddervolds Square and spread out the map to see where I was going. These maps are for free, it's great. I always keep one folded in a plastic bag under my saddle, so I can get about. You're smiling non-stop, Johanne, I said to myself. I had to bring my fingers up to my face, to touch my lips, to touch the joy. Do I have dimples? Stop this nonsense, I said, becoming stern with myself. I found the street, planned the route in my head, put the map back, sat on my bike and pedalled off. I sang as I cycled. I wasn't sure of the lyrics, but it didn't matter. My home is where my Lord is, that's where I belong. I was happy. I felt it in every part of me. I wished I could cycle all night and never arrive.

The pee in the bucket is dark and concentrated. It smells. The clouds are gathering outside. I think it'll rain. I reached 160-something sit-ups, then lost count. I'm taking a break, lying on my back with my legs up doing nothing. You probably have to lie like this to keep the sperm inside when you want to fall pregnant. I should shout from the window now and get somebody to call

Mum at work. But I don't. It's as though I haven't got the strength. Perhaps I'm locked in here as part of an experiment. Perhaps somebody's pumping gases in and changing my consciousness. The very thought of lifting my legs exhausts me. I'm annoyed at Ivar. I think he could have helped me more. He should have fetched me. Made a firmer arrangement. This open invitation was a nonsense. Maybe he'd had second thoughts and decided he didn't really want me to come after all. So this casual invitation was just a good way of getting out of it.

You must be Johanne, said a girl at the door. Ivar asked me to look out for you. I nodded, said hello and smiled. She didn't smile back. I wondered what Ivar had said that meant she could recognize me. Slightly plump, red hair, a bit different. Suddenly she broke into a broad smile. She had dimples and was prettier than any girl I'd seen up at Blindern. Happier. Wide trousers, an old faded T-shirt, a greeny-blue colour, and nice round boobs. Still smiling, she looked at me. I looked down at my long baggy dress. We were standing in the doorway of a factory building. A large sheet hung on the wall next to the entrance covered in red writing. It had shone out at me as I came down the hill. There were burning torches on tall stands either side of the door. I locked my bike to a signpost. The girl waited. She had nothing on except her tight top, but didn't seem to feel the cold. Come on, she said, let's go. She was so friendly, I didn't know how to interpret it. I just wanted to see Ivar, to see his hair, his skinny arms, his hands and eyes. I wished everyone else would go away, so he and I could be alone. It hadn't occurred to me that this party was for anyone else. I'd only imagined the two of us. I wanted this pretty girl to disappear. We went along a black corridor. At the end was a piece of red velvet, draped like a curtain in an arc with a sash. It all felt like a movie, a fantasy: multicoloured drapes, shifting melodies, disparate music, moans and noises. Golden-brown girls, grimy, standing about, leaning on the wall, broad mouths smiling, licking their lips. My nipples were hard. Someone had whipped my back tight. I went over to the entrance and peeped in.

Smoke was making the light foggy, the music invaded my spine, it was all too strident and loud, clumping together to make a tight, broad belt that enclosed everything. People sat about, stood, talked, laughed. Dust everywhere, filling nostrils. Glass rinsers churning. Water splashing into a dirty steel sink. And this hazy light. I couldn't see any band. The music was on cassette or CD or some kind of tape in an old stereo system, crackling. Wasn't Ivar meant to play? He'd asked me to come here. He was waiting for me in another room. Or a dark corridor. My breasts burned, as though someone had sliced off my nipples. I thought of Mum and wondered what I'd tell her. Yes, Mum, we all stood in a circle and held hands. I leant against the wall and closed my eyes. Ivar is watching me through a one-way mirror. He can see how useless I am. He's standing there with a friend. He's told him all about me. They are holding a beer each. They're drinking it straight from the bottle. Ivar is smoking. He takes a drag and exhales. Takes another swig. They both look at me, then at each other. Ivar says something and they laugh.

Johanne! It was his voice. I've been waiting for you. I began to think you weren't coming. Then Lise told me you arrived ages ago. He was in a dressing gown, naked underneath. I glimpsed his dark pubic hair, but couldn't see his dick. Aren't you well? he asked. Sure, I said. Have you taken something? he said. No, I said. I had to smile: he was at it too now. His voice seemed to float, so deep it felt as though it reached inside me from below. I felt the long, heavy dress around my thighs, a chafing at my skin, a tingling. I didn't want it to stop. Johanne, he said, can't you open your eyes and look at me? His eyes were grotesquely big, like one of those dogs in the fairy tale. His hands and lips were swollen. I opened my eyes. He was the same as usual, just more handsome. Kindly, joyous, sad eyes. The band weren't going to play after all. One of the boys had had to go and see his sister, who'd fallen ill, but Ivar was here with me. He wanted us to dance. His trousers were thin, so was his shirt, all his clothes were thin, and we went into a corner, and he stroked my back, and I let my hands wander over his body, he was like water, like light on a rocky pool, flashing, sharp, abrupt. I've never gone to bed with anyone before, I said.

It was dark. I saw the little red light on the TV. We were in his apartment. A studio flat with a big window and a narrow mattress. Ivar stood right in front of me, close to me. My ears were still buzzing from the music. I looked at him. He said nothing, he smiled softly, took my hand and squeezed it, laid it against his cheek. I always thought I'd wait until the time was right. But how do we know when it's right? I knew I wanted to do it, so it would simply have to be right. We were going to do it and it was as if I'd known for ages, as if it had been decided on that day with the towel. Ivar whispered something in my ear, I didn't hear what. Then he was in the bathroom, busy with something. I had no idea what. There was light coming through the window, from the street lamp below. I had decided to let tonight be an exception, a parenthesis. I would take time off, a holiday. I had to allow myself this, permit myself these experiences. I might need them in the future, in my work, with some client. Ivar returned to the room and put on some music I didn't know, a continuation of what we'd danced to at the party, but softer. He took a blue box down from a shelf, opened it and took out a tiny flat packet – a sweet? He walked over to me, looked at me seriously, as though by standing like that he was saying something, as if we were making a new agreement. He tucked the sachet behind his ear, inclined his head and smiled. I saw it was a condom. I didn't know what to say. I felt them coming over me. The tears. He asked me what the matter was. I don't know, I said, I just suddenly feel like crying. I sat on the mattress. He went down on his knees in front of me, pushed my legs apart and knelt there between them, close to me. He held my face in his hands, sucked the tears away, began to lick my face, my eyelids, my temples, like the warm tongue of a little dog. That wags its tail, I thought later, as he poked his sex against my entrance and pushed. And I felt how it opened to let him in. It hurt a bit, but every time he withdrew, I was frightened he might never come inside again.

I remember an Easter holiday in the mountains. We were lost and days passed without our knowing where we were. I was skiing behind a pulk sled. It was foggy and windy and all I could see was the triangular patterns my skis made as they touched the back of the sled in front. These imprints, I thought, were the mountains we had to cross, and new ones kept appearing, endlessly. I was nine years old and I was convinced I'd never see my mother again. This would be my last ski trip and Mum wasn't there. And we had the puppy with us too. It was only a few weeks old, round, fluffy and joyful. It was soon exhausted, padding through the snow with its little paws. I felt so sorry for it. Its little paws in the biting, wet snow. Did it bleed perhaps? I seem to remember that it bled, that tracks of blood appeared in the snow. If only I could go back now, I'd have taken better care of it, made a sling from my scarf and carried it on my back. Or had a rucksack so it could sit and peer out. I wonder if Ivar has ever had a dog. He wanted me to stay already that first night. Just to be there. But it was an impossibility. A brick wall. I had to go home so Mum wouldn't worry about me, so things didn't get blown out of proportion. I'd made up my mind that tonight was a holiday. Not tomorrow. Not any other day. Yet it seemed impossible to stop holding this hard, warm body close. I remember staring at the ceiling, everything was a blur since I'd taken my glasses off, in the soft light coming in from the street lamp and the cars outside, it shifted, edges melted away. Everything became one. I thought of God, that he was here too. Everything was here. It was like dying, I thought. And I began to cry again, harder this time. I didn't understand why, why it came over me every time my joy felt complete. Thinking about it now, I cry again. What is it with me? I wanted to do it one more time before I left. I was afraid I might forget how it felt. I have to sleep with you every day, I said, my body needs you. Once an hour, said Ivar, smiling. He was lying on his stomach resting on his elbows, playing with my hair, lining up the curls, until he finally put them in a heap over my eyes so I couldn't see anything.

Come with me to America, he said. Yes, I said. In two weeks' time, he said. All right, I said, and laughed at this wild fantasy, this fantastical dream; the two of us in Central Park, on Broadway. We lay on our backs and stared up at the ceiling. There's dust floating everywhere, I thought, and it is falling on us right now, turning us into a memory. I mean it, said Ivar. Really? I said. I imagined us on a plane together. Taking off. My brother's studying at MIT, I said, about to tell him more about Edvard. I mean it, Johanne. It'll be great. You can just bring your books. I've saved up some money and we'll live cheaply in a little place south of Pittsburgh, Pennsylvania, you can study and I'll play guitar. I didn't answer. I was picturing us driving down wide streets, sitting in warm diners, eating muffins and fried eggs, sleeping with each other several times a day, waking up together, laughing, showering, splashing in the bath together. My mouth had gone dry. I got up and went to the kitchen, found a glass in the cupboard, turned on the tap. I looked out of the window into the dark backyard. Everything was so filthy, so run-down. I imagined another kitchen. I was forty and sitting at a Formica table on a hot, dirty Los Angeles day, drinking gin. It was noon. I looked a wreck, my face was saggy; a long-haired black dog lay asleep under the table, my feet resting on its coat. A fly buzzed around. I was looking out of the window at the cars going past. Inside another window, the round one, I saw the slender, clever, beautiful woman, the one with her hand on the telephone receiver, who cast a warm, thoughtful glance towards the garden, and saw her next client coming in through the gate and walking beneath an avenue of birches bursting into leaf. I longed for her, that slim, calm woman, and if I just kept a grip on my plan, I thought, she could become a reality. I would be that woman.

I went out into the lounge and found my clothes. Ivar lay on the mattress and watched me as I dressed. Neither of us said anything, which was good. I wanted to get home as quickly as possible. Fortunately everything had gone well, but the remains of my future had to be rescued. We had been running and playing on a high plateau, and only now had we reached the edge and become aware of the abyss. He followed me to the door. He was naked. I knelt down and gave his soft penis a parting kiss. I got up and put my hand on the door handle; he held me under the chin and looked at me very seriously. My back seemed to stiffen again as we stood looking at each other.

I had turned off the alarm and now I switched it back on from inside. The little light on the control panel came on. I stood in the dark hall. It smelt of home. I was aware that my body was still somehow permeated with what had just happened. I had to be quiet so as not to wake Mum up. I went into the bathroom, looked at myself in the mirror. My hands shook as I lifted a cotton-wool ball with make-up remover on it. I heard a floorboard creak in the lounge. I'd woken her up after all. I remembered a ghost story – when you looked at a person behind you in the mirror, they were revealed in their true form, as a good spirit or a devil. The door handle turned, I closed my eyes and swung round, holding the cotton wool over my left eye. I opened my eyes. She was wearing a skimpy, see-through negligee. She said nothing. She looked in the mirror, as though she'd been lying in bed thinking about her appearance and had had to rush to the bathroom to check it out. Then she looked at me. I felt sure everything was visible, everything I'd done, and that I'd wanted it, all of it, and that I'd had fun. I thought you were asleep, I said. She looked at me sadly, as though I was a disappointment.

I stared down at the floor and went on wiping off my make-up. Johanne, she said, in a wafer-thin voice. I knew I'd done something wrong, or forgotten something terribly important. I looked at her legs and remembered that I'd promised to wax them, she doesn't know how to do it, and it was several days since we had talked about it. I can do them for you now, I said. What are you talking about? she said. Your leg wax, I said. She said nothing, just sat down on the toilet seat while I fetched her cigarettes and lighter, a clean towel and a stool for her to put her feet up on. As I prepared the wax, I thought about the massive benefits I had living here, not having to rent a place, and all the money I saved, and how lucky I was.

How did it go at Granny's? Mum asked. You haven't told me yet. It was fine, I said. She refused to talk about the alarm, but she was glad to see me. What should I do, Johanne? Why is she so angry with me? Mum asked. I knelt on the floor and spread the wax as carefully as I could, trying to console her with the gentleness of my touch. My mind was drifting, I couldn't answer her, couldn't focus on what she said, it all felt so infinitely boring. She's not senile, I said. She has to be allowed to make her own decisions. She's doing it to punish me, said Mum, she doesn't want to make me happy.

The idea of making someone happy always makes me think of altruism. There's an entire chapter devoted to it in my social psychology textbook. Discussing the extent to which we do things for others, without any thought of personal advantage. Even fascists, a few at least, are known to have rescued Jews during the war. They usually made the decision to help on impulse, in situations of extreme pressure. The key unifying factor among these people seems to be that they themselves had been shown compassion at some time; the urge to be protective had been learnt through experience and become a spontaneous, natural reaction.

Is the latch stiffer than usual? I've decided to open the window. But now it's jammed and I can't. Fucking stupid window. Language, Johanne, watch yourself. I've got the sheet wrapped round me, so it probably looks like a towel from a distance, completely normal. There now, it's open. I had to give it a thump in the bottom corner. The air is cool, colder than it looks. A blast of wind fills the room. I lean forward and look down at the asphalt.

Ivar's invited me on a trip to the US, I said. I was sitting there on the bathroom floor and it just came out. I hadn't planned to say it. I hadn't actually given it any proper thought yet, this extraordinary offer from Ivar. It wasn't something I could rely on and trust, it was too fragile. And yet I said it. Mum didn't reply. She just looked at me and took a drag on her cigarette, held it hard against her lips, then took another deep drag. I'd pressed a clean strip of muslin onto her leg, and we were waiting for the wax to grip properly. A trip. For how long? she asked. Six weeks, I said. Ivar had given me the impression that it might be longer, but I didn't mention that. I see, she said eventually. And where exactly are you going in the US? she asked. I'm going to Pennsylvania, I said, somewhere near Pittsburgh. I regretted saying it. I should have waited until I was more sure. Putting words to it seemed to push me so much closer to my departure, made me feel somehow more obliged to go, and at the same time wiped out my desire. It suddenly just seemed odd. Travelling in the middle of term, with a man I'd only just met? Putting my whole future in jeopardy, when I'd just started out on a six-and-a-half-year study programme? I could hear how daft it sounded. I wanted to tell her I was joking, but Mum seemed so fragile. If I stirred things up more now, she'd just get angry. We leave on Thursday, in two weeks, I said, trying to sound confident.

That night I awoke from a dream that I still remember with absolute clarity. It began in a school playground. I was sitting with two other kids at a table by the wall of the school building. It must have been break time, we were playing cards. My family were living on the first floor. It was a hot, sunny day and the windows of the apartment were open above us. Suddenly we heard groaning from the bedroom window. I recognized the sound of my mother's intense pleasure, it was already loud and I knew it would even get louder. I had to persuade them to close the window. I put my cards down on the table and made a joke about having to protect my family honour. The other two kids looked at me and smiled wryly. I walked round the building, went in and up the stairs. As I approached the bedroom I saw that it didn't have its usual veneer door, but an old blue-painted door with a large glass panel in the middle. I couldn't avoid seeing in. I saw Mum lying on her back across the bed with a duvet over her. Her ankles were tied to the crossbars of the window. Standing next to her was a man. I could see him clearly. Mum was completely covered by the duvet, her eyes included, but somehow I could still see her mouth. I hadn't known this was what they were doing. Bondage. From outside it had sounded as though she'd been enjoying it. Now I saw her lips moving. Saying that she wasn't used to being treated like a child, that she wanted him to treat her like an adult. All I wanted was for them to shut the window. Then I'd leave as fast possible. I had to knock for ages before they heard me. Suddenly Mum flung the duvet away from her eyes, and looking at me, upside down, through the glass, she realized it was me. Then weeping, she said, Just let her come in, so she can see what her father does to me.

It all seemed incredibly simple the next morning. Everything was possible, even America, everything was open and light and far in the future. It was easy to get out of bed and to get going. My body felt strong. Coming out of the shower, I looked at my arms in the mirror. My muscles suddenly had more definition, seemed more prominent. Despite going to bed late the night before, I wasn't at all tired. I remember thinking I'd needed less sleep and that it maybe had something to do with sex. I smiled all the way to Blindern. I can see myself now on my yellow bicycle. Yes, I was happy. I almost crashed into Terje at the corner, near the Theology block, as he came down from Sogn. We laughed and waved and cycled on in our separate ways. Riding past the Portakabins at the broadcasting building, I suddenly felt a strange longing to kiss Terje. I wanted to kiss everyone I liked, every man – thin, fat, young or old – they had all grown beautiful and I desired each and every one of them.

I locked my bike up on the rack, climbed the stairs to the reading room and waited with everyone else. Could they see what had happened to me? I went in. My mouth refused to stop smiling. I put my books on my desk, wrote an 'occupied' note and went downstairs. I was a diva in a movie. I felt so beautiful: my hair flowing, a mass of curls, my skirt heavy and feminine. When I think back, I'm glad no one saw me, no one I knew at least. Lord above. It must have been obvious to anyone who saw. I moved as though I was in a melody. I headed straight for the kitchen, past the dirty dishes, shy of nothing. Ivar was over by the extractor fan, smoking with his back to me. I was his woman. I remember thinking it. I am your woman, Ivar, I said. I tried to say it in a deep, sensual voice. He turned, saw me, looked at me and smiled. A smile that came from deep inside him, warm and knowing. Still looking at me, he flicked the ash with his fingers and walked towards me. I felt his every move in my legs, in my belly, he only had to make the merest gesture and I sensed him inside me. I looked at him, the bulge in his trousers, the short white jacket, the sleeves folded back, showing his forearms. Then he kissed me, touching my arse, both hands on my butt as we kissed, and I was so strong, that's what strikes me now, how strong I felt. I barely recognize myself. He looked down at me with questioning eyes. I knew what he was asking and I answered with a nod. Yes, I said. I loved saying yes to him. I adored it. He took a key from a cupboard, told one of the others that he had to fetch something. The other guy smiled. All three of us smiled. I remember feeling it was OK, it must have been the sense of elation, the fact that I was so happy, and, yes, that I was so turned on, and that it was somehow all right, it suddenly felt completely fine and it didn't matter if anyone else knew. We went down into the basement, down the stairs, hugging each other. I insisted on walking behind him, holding him round the middle, and we nearly tumbled over. Shh, he said to me sternly. I just laughed. In one of the underground corridors he unlocked a door. We went inside and he locked it after us. The room was dusty, stacked full of tables and chairs. I started undoing Ivar's belt and pulled down his trousers. Stay still, I said. I don't know where I'd got the idea. The soft skin on his hard penis, smooth and lovely. It was so good. I'd never done it before, but I was hungry, that was how it felt. I wanted to be closely acquainted with his genitals. To tease and caress him. I ate him. Chewed and sucked. I told him to sit down. We smiled. Ivar sat on a chair, an old school chair, or kitchen chair. He looked sweet with his prick standing up against his belly. I pulled down my skirt, my tights, my knickers. My inner thighs were soaking, I didn't know it was possible to be so wet. I sat over him. I could. It seemed completely natural now. He leant his head back towards the leg of a table that had been stacked upside down. He looked at me, eyes half shut. I didn't know which entered me, his gaze or his prick. I moved slowly up and down. I felt my own sex like a tight ring. He stroked my buttocks. Then he took my waist so hard I had to stop, he looked at me, and for a moment we were silent. I love you, he said. All I wanted was to move on him again. To go on and on. And he touched me as though he knew my body blindfold. I think we made lots of noise. I remember my belly against a large, cold table, my breasts tingling. It was so beautiful. I suppose that was why I cried so much afterwards. I curled up in a little ball in his lap and he blew on my neck. I'm starting to cry again now, here in this stupid blue room. Ivar, Ivar. To think I'll never have sex with you again.

My face is completely wet. I wish I had a tissue to dry my eyes and blow my nose on. I use the sheet. Why not? It hardly matters; a pink sheet in this blue room, utterly meaningless. I wipe my nose, rub my cheeks hard. I don't want anyone to find me like this. Why am I crying when it's all over? Ivar will have left by now, it's gone eleven, it'll be twelve soon, I'm gaining nothing. It's like the autumn with its wind and leaves and rain, bathing everything, washing the world clean. If something can be blown away, disappear so quickly, was it nothing? Can I have any measure of what has been in the now? What is the now? Why are my most trivial memories the clearest? The way he held his cigarette between his fingers that Saturday morning, when I'd stayed overnight after all, the way he cradled it in his hand like a warm potato on a blustery day; and his gaze out of the window, distant, stern. Those times when he looked angry. He was so handsome then. Hard, severe. Have I forgotten him in just these few hours? Is it possible that he's completely gone from inside me? But what if he hasn't and I still have him somewhere inside me, beneath every thought, like a broad river flowing hot under a crust of cold thoughts, tearing at the river bank, so that its sands crash into the water, so that any edges in me crumble away without my knowledge. Who am I then? How can I be sure what I know? How can I know what is real?

That Tuesday I was working like a madwoman, with total focus, as a prepayment so I could spend the evening with Ivar. If I studied hard enough it would be all right. I was coming back from the toilets, when I saw Karin emerge from the reading room. I don't think she saw me, but I got the feeling she'd gone there hoping to find me. I let her walk away. Thinking of it now, I see God walking down the spiral staircase beside her; the two of them – a strong Karin and a fragile, transparent figure in conversation. God is sad and Karin turns to him and smiles, baring lovely teeth. Karin's smile makes everybody happy. She should just stand at the altar and smile, and that would be blessing enough. Dear Father, be with Karin – she deserves it. What kind of dreadful notion, Johanne, to deserve God. Forgive me, Lord, I didn't mean it like that.

I remember Ivar bowed over the lock of his shiny bicycle. He turns his head towards me, ostrich-like, and smiles. The yellow light from the fridge in the Co-op shining on his face, his freckles, his glance, those blue eyes. He is holding up a packet of cheese. This one? I think it was raining that afternoon. Yes, I remember his cold lips and hot breath under the hood of his raincoat, and how it dripped on us out in the backyard, just down there, before we came in, and the things he said, how I poked fun at his dialect as we made the food, how he turned and pointed the kitchen knife at me, you know something, Johanne, it's a good job I've got this. I couldn't help telling him how one of the boys in my class had told us a story in the cookery class, about a woman who'd had two fists stuck up her at once. So that's the kind of thing you go about remembering, Johanne. That's very bad. He smiled, shook his head and sighed. Sometimes I wonder what you actually dream about, what you really want. He grabbed my wrists and pulled me to him, and we laughed and kissed, and I knew that if we'd been alone, we'd have done it there and then. Actually we were alone, but Mum could arrive any minute. I touched him through his apron. My hand seemed so small and fragile, I'd never felt that before, and I remember I was happy at being weaker than him. We were standing like that when I heard Mum's key in the door. And it struck me that I'd forgotten to tell her that Ivar was eating with us. Strange that I'd forgotten. I could easily have rung, but I hadn't. She was generally pleased when I brought people home, most often Karin, but I suddenly felt sure she wouldn't be so eager to meet Ivar. I don't know if the thought or the feeling came first, they seemed to come simultaneously. I wanted to hurry the cooking up, but when I reached out for the saucepan I felt a pain shoot up my back. It was as though the muscles had contracted and refused to release.

Why are we incapable of helping ourselves with these things? Why can't we massage our own body? Stroke our own back with warm hands? I opened my eyes and you looked at me. We were lying close together on the narrow mattress. It was the middle of the night. I don't know whether you'd been sleeping. We didn't smile, just looked at each other, smiles somehow deep within. When I think now, when I close my eyes, we're back there. You open your eyes and I'm lying there watching you. Neither of us says a word. It's like a hot liquid flowing in and filling gaps I never knew existed.

Hello, darling, Mum shouted, as she opened the front door. I went out into the hall and gave her a hug. I don't know why, I don't usually. Mum must have seen Ivar's shoes, or noticed something. Have we got a visitor? She was smiling as she said it. I recall a summer job I had in a street kiosk. I was serving a woman with fruit, green apples I think, and as I turned to her after weighing them I must have gone faint or something, because my customer suddenly seemed to reveal her true face. Her skin had only been a disguise, now her cheeks were covered with rough fur and scars and her tongue lolled out between her teeth. Ivar's here, I said. You can meet each other. She stiffened slightly, and paused to take off her scarf, the long rust-coloured one that goes round her neck several times. I'd have liked to say he hadn't come here to exploit us, that Ivar had his own money and could buy food for himself, that he lived alone and had done so for years. But I'd paid for the food with Mum's card. They shook hands. I remember thinking Ivar might have smiled a little more broadly, made a better first impression, been more giving, so she'd see he wasn't dangerous. He could make an effort, I thought. I saw Mum's negative reaction to him, to the fact that he didn't hold her gaze long enough, I wanted to tell him to look her in the eye. It upset me that he didn't bother, didn't understand. Something so simple, so elementary. Was he an idiot? Mum went into her room behind the curtain to change and then into the bathroom. I could feel where she was in the apartment through my back. Ivar and I went quiet, and carried on making the food. He held me round the waist and wanted to tickle and kiss me, but I didn't laugh. I was concentrating, concerned that everything should be as nice as possible and look good. Candles, serviettes, tableware perfectly laid out on the table, a casual symmetry. Maybe I should put some classical music on. I went into the lounge and took out the Satie.

Where do they come from, the things we do? When do they become a part us, a quirk, a hallmark? I don't know. All too early, I'd say. Every spring, on Constitution Day, my brother and I were given fifty kroner to spend at the funfair. Edvard would use all his up straight away. I'd save mine. I'd trail around with the adults and they'd pay to see me on an occasional ride or to do a lucky dip – I didn't need to spend a thing. I often felt rather sorry for Edvard when his money was gone. I was ashamed that I never gave him any of mine. I know he thought I was boring and mean, he'd look right past me, not even bothering to pull a long face. I have no idea what I was saving for. I only remember the act of saving itself, watching the coin counter on my piggybank rising steadily, like a thermometer, it was a good feeling. Why does it cost so much to survive? It's impossible to do without, we're caught in a cycle, money has to come from somewhere, there'll always be somebody who produces money and a hand to stretch out and take it. My hand, my fingers. I look down at them. They're puny and weak. I fold them, they're cold and feel alien to each other. Teach me to give, O Father, as You have given me life and happiness. Teach me to be more like You.

Mum sat in the lounge with the evening paper. We could hear her leafing through it over the piano music. We'd finished preparing the meal, a simple dish, pasta with tomato sauce, vegetarian; at least she couldn't accuse me of wasting money on meat. Ivar had wanted to pay in the shop, but I'd argued that he was the visitor. And then I'd paid on Mum's card. Johanne, Johanne, you have only yourself to thank. I shouted out to her that the food was ready. I heard the leather chair creak as she got up. Ivar went out into the hall as she came into the kitchen. We were alone. Mum said nothing, but seemed upset. What's the matter? I asked. She frowned and stared at me intensely, as though trying to say something without words. Is he good enough for you? Or something of the sort. I didn't want to reveal that I knew what she meant, and answered by raising my eyebrows in feigned confusion, and then Ivar walked back into the kitchen. He must have noticed the expression on my face and felt he'd interrupted us in a very private conversation, since he looked at me with that warm expression of his, as if to ask if everything was all right. I smiled back. Keen to get on, I told Mum she could sit down and I'd serve. I stood with my back to them and filled the water jug. When I turned there was a bottle of wine on the table. So that was what Ivar had gone to fetch from the hall. I'd have given anything for it to disappear. He didn't know what was good for him. Coming here with a bottle of wine. Mum looked at me as if she was checking how I reacted, if I'd known about the wine, if it had been my idea. I popped into the Vinmonopolet today, Ivar said, when I was out in the van picking up some stock for work. He smiled at us both. Mum doesn't drink; she doesn't like the taste. She smiled faintly. That was kind of you, she said. Wasn't it, Johanne? Great, I said. I hadn't realized he had such a relaxed attitude to alcohol on a weekday. I was suddenly unsure about him. Who was he really? Would he start drinking? Would he ever get a proper job? I saw us living in a caravan, dirty, cramped and messy. I put the saucepan on the table, took off the lid; it smelt deliciously of basil and garlic. So what's the special occasion? Mum asked, leaning forward with a smile. Then it occurred to me that she wasn't too fond of pasta. Why did I always forget these things, when my memory was otherwise so good? She looked at me and smiled. I tried to work out what that smile really meant. Ivar asked for a corkscrew. I got up to find it. We've got one with a green-painted handle that I bought at a jumble sale. I was surprised he hadn't noticed anything, that he didn't realize he'd made a mistake bringing the wine. But he was probably a bit nervous too.

I had to try to see the situation from his perspective, try to help him. Suddenly my back seized up. It felt ready to snap completely if I so much as leant forward too quickly. The pain was so strong, I couldn't think about anything else. Mum looked out of the window. Ivar looked at me. I wished he'd look the other way. Keep to himself and stop leaning towards me like that. I was grateful for the music and that I'd remembered to put it on. I opened the wine, fetched three stem glasses and poured it out. Ivar lifted his glass, to make a toast. I raised mine vaguely and drank. We served ourselves and started to eat. When I looked up from the table again, Mum was staring straight at Ivar. She'd clearly been watching him for a while. There was silence, the cheerful piano waltz had just come to an end, and Ivar was concentrating on getting a pasta twist onto his fork. Tell me about love, Ivar, said Mum. He looked up at her and then at me. What do you mean? he said. He put his food in his mouth and started to chew. Mum didn't answer. She just looked at him with her head cocked to one side, smiling seriously. Ivar looked from her to me again. He seemed bewildered. The essence of love, she said. The true nature of love. She said the word love slowly and solemnly, giving the 'l' an extra lilt. Is this some kind of interrogation? said Ivar. I could hear he was trying to be humorous, but Mum clearly didn't notice his light-hearted tone. No, she said, looking straight at him again. I hoped he'd be able to hold her gaze. Love is an attempt, she searched for the words, an attempt to share our sense of wonder at the greatest mystery in life.

Giving him a meaningful glance, she turned to look out of the window and then took a sip of her wine – after all. She smiled to herself and shook her head, as though she was musing on an answer somebody else had once given to this question, long ago. When Mum had posed it to Karin, she'd simply answered that love was God and God was love. Then they'd gazed at each other for a long time, as though they were wrapped in the same thoughts, sharing its spell, so happy they couldn't bear to move. Tears had welled up in Mum's eyes, they'd hugged each other and Karin had stroked her back. Mum has never asked me. I don't know what I'd reply. It's one of those white areas of thought, or rather a black hole into which all thoughts vanish.

I look down at my watch. At the second hand moving round and round. That, I think, is my life disappearing. Every time it moves I draw a little closer to death. I love the blue colour I painted this room with. So clear and pure. I feel like we belong together. That it's my most loyal friend. But can it know that? Is it aware that it is loved by me? Can that give it any comfort, or make it feel less alone?

I was in the kitchen drinking tea. It was dark. I'd been sitting there for a long time. I hadn't switched any lights on. I'd considered lighting a candle, but I just sat there, staring out of the window. My thoughts drifted, they were transparent, thin veils, and from behind them Ivar came into view. He was rehearsing with the band again. He'd asked me to take his key, to be at home for him when he got back, to sleep over. I couldn't. I'd said I needed to go to bed early, to catch up on my sleep. He'd held me hard and said, No naughtiness, you hear, and kissed me on the forehead. I like that sort of firmness, the way he held me, his stern voice, the way he grabbed me without asking permission, helping himself. I could hear her footsteps in the backyard below, as the front gate closed, the clacking on the paving stones, the downstairs door slamming, the sound of her walking up the stairs. She turned the light on in the hallway, glanced at herself in the mirror, then looked into the kitchen. Oh, you're sitting in here, she said. Mum dropped her handbag onto the floor, kicked off her shoes and put her jacket on a hanger. I couldn't see her from where I was sitting, I could just hear her movements, her voice: Johanne, I need to talk to you. She went into the bathroom. I heard her pee. She came straight out again without washing her hands. I was about to remind her to wash them – after all, she'd been out touching all kinds of things. I didn't. What did she want to talk to me about? She walked on through the lounge and behind the curtain. I heard her open her wardrobe. She was changing her clothes. What did you want to say? I shouted. There was no reply. I went over to the cooker, turned on the hotplate to warm the vegetable soup: carrots, potatoes and kohlrabi, one stock cube, garlic and a squeeze of tomato purée, the healthiest and cheapest option, less than twenty kroner for two. Mum came out of her room and stopped in the hallway to put on her indoor shoes. I stirred the soup. We looked at each other. I went back to my chair and sat down. Here it comes, I thought. Here comes the moment of judgement. Johanne, said Mum. She took a glass from the cupboard, fetched a bottle of Diet Coke from the fridge, poured it out and drank. Ah, I was thirsty, she said. She looked at me and attempted to smile. What did you want to say? I asked. Johanne, she said, sitting down. She lifted the lid of her Winnertip cigarette-making machine, tucked some pinches of tobacco in the groove and distributed them evenly. She paused and looked at me. I shouldn't burden you with this, she said, fixing an empty cigarette shell in place, closing the flap and pushing the tobacco in. Click-clack. I lifted my teacup slowly. The tea was cold and there were only a few drops left at the bottom. I took a sip, held the empty cup to my mouth. Mum lit her cigarette and gazed out of the window. She seemed sad. Poor Mum. I thought about everything she'd been through, I wanted to be nice to her, to look after her. She opened her mouth as if to say something, but stopped midway. Then she said, I've been thinking about painting the lounge. We need a bit of colour with the long dark evenings closing in. Don't you think, Johanne? Yes, I said, we certainly do. That's a great idea, Mum. Johanne dear, I know you're busy with all your studies, but do you think you could take it in hand? We're so busy at work. Sure, I said, of course I can. She wanted me to select the shade, I'd drop by the hardware store and pick up a colour chart; it didn't take long for us to decide on yellow, we needed a warm sunny colour for the cold winter days. She took a little soup, added more salt, ate and smiled. I was glad she was happy. We agreed that I'd make some new sofa cushion covers too; some plain and others patterned with touches of yellow. That would cheer things up. We had a lovely evening. I remember feeling happy as I went to bed, pleased that we were back on good terms and that she'd stopped being angry with me. Everything was going to be fine, and I could stay here until I'd completed my studies.

I think of the days Ivar and I have spent together. Almost two weeks up until now. Each day has been a little life. I've got up and cycled to Blindern. Taken my place in the reading room, opened my books, looked at the ceiling and sent a smile up to God. Studied hard. Everything has been exciting and interesting. I've done my reading on schizophrenia. I've started on depression, and a new chapter in my social psychology book called *Loving, Liking and Close Relationships*. My books are in my bag out in the hall.

I see Ivar in a hundred double exposures. I see his body in his white jacket and tatty blue jeans, he moves in my imagination, a flower bursting forth. He turns to me, goes down on one knee and asks if I'll accompany him to the record store. He sits, stands, walks about in his apartment, a sandwich in one hand, talking at me with a full mouth. We hurtle along on our bikes, in the rain, his brown hair flying straight back. In the evening, he lies on his stomach on the mattress in front of an old Bergman film on TV, he must have been watching me for a long time without my noticing. He crosses the reading room towards me, hips gyrating crudely, hand at his crotch, index finger straight up, and we laugh. His teeth. His lips. The water dripping from his chin in the shower. He takes my glasses off, pushes my hair from my forehead, runs his fingers deep in my curls. His eyes when he looks at me from below as he kisses my breasts. My child, sweet little thing. And when he's inside me, just before he comes, his face contorts as though the skin were suddenly too tight, as though he were sobbing, a look of boundless despair. It was a battle every night, to be allowed to sleep at home. One evening I went to meet him, to surprise him outside his rehearsal venue. An old factory with grimy windows. I sat on the pavement next to my bike, near the wall by the door, with a book he wanted me to read, a short Norwegian novel about a lighthouse keeper's family out on an island. I had decided to go to America with Ivar, but I didn't want to tell him, in case I couldn't go for some reason. A couple of junkies came walking along the pavement, a man and a woman. She was wearing a short pink skirt and navy stockings. When they'd gone, I imagined the two of us like that. If I wasn't careful I'd turn into her and Ivar would be my pimp. I felt my anger start to rise. He wanted to pressurize me into things. He was pushing me beyond my limits, bit by bit, nudging me further all the time. Just being here, waiting for him, sitting on a filthy pavement in Grünerløkka, was a step too far. Moments later Ivar came out of the door with the rest of the band. One of them suggested going to Schous for a beer. Ivar was happy to see me, or seemed to be. He crouched in front of me and kissed me on the forehead, cheeks, nose and mouth. Come with us for a drink, he said. I didn't want to, but said nothing. These ambitionless, layabout friends of his, going for a beer on an ordinary Wednesday night. Couldn't he see how vulnerable he was making us? It was like selling yourself. Lying down and exposing yourself to everything destructive. Ivar said we should pick up my bike on the way back. I locked it up carefully. He held my hand, but with the pavement being so narrow I ended up trailing behind him. How can you put up with this, Johanne? I thought. You're like a sheep, a little pink piggy on a lead. The air was thick with cigarette smoke down in this dive, I'd never been here before, it was dark, dirty and shabby. I wanted to leave immediately, but I sat there with a cup of tea, Ivar's foot touching mine under the table, his warmth holding me captive. Half an hour later I got up, saying that I had a headache and had to leave. Ivar got up too. He took some money from his pocket and put it on the table for his beer and my tea. The band smiled, one of boys made a comment I didn't catch, and they all laughed. Ivar smiled back. I assumed it was something obscene. My girl, he whispered into my hair as we headed for the exit. Opening the door for me with one hand, he took me round the waist. I thought you'd stay with them, I said, as we came out. I wouldn't have minded, you know, I don't own you. It was cold, the air was damp. A tram rumbled past. Ivar tried to say something. What? I said. He stopped, took my face in his hands and placed his forehead against mine. Are you nuts, Johanne? Are you out of your mind? You think I'd let you go like that? he said. We looked at each other. His eyes were so close that they glided into one. I only want to be where you are.

And where are you now, Ivar? I stand by the window and look out. Somewhere up there in the sky? Why can't someone take care of me? Johanne! You seem to think you can put the responsibility for your life into other people's hands. Love yourself. Come on now. I can't sit down here. Can't slump passively into a chair when I'm about to burst, to shoot out of this room, like a little cold pebble, the kind you find in their thousands on the beach, that you pick up and rub and weigh in your palm, before dropping it to rejoin the others. I kick the door but it hurts my foot. I ought to throw the chair into it, smash it open, make a hole in it. Why don't I? Am I worried about the damage? The cost? I have approximately eighty kroner in my purse. That won't stretch to anything. I've got 26,319 kroner in the savings account for my apartment. Laughable. Derisory, Johanne. Pathetic. You are standing still. You'll never get on in life. You're incapable of anything.

The next evening I left the colour chart on the table, before going to meet Ivar. Mum hadn't come home yet. Then we'd discussed it one morning, a day or so later,

Mum wasn't quite satisfied with any of the shades I'd picked out. Oh dear, she said, looking up at me, I'm wearing you out. I smiled, filled my Thermos with coffee, tore off a piece of greaseproof paper for my packed lunch. It's no problem, Mum, practical things like that are fun. The following Saturday I mixed a yellow from my watercolour box. We both liked it, a strong, warm colour. I put the sample I'd made in her purse, and we agreed that she'd order the paint during her lunch break and have it delivered.

I want to imagine Ivar and me. To think of us when we make love. When we're lying next to each other, our bodies close. I want my thoughts to be beautiful, because it was never anything but beautiful, and we deserve it. We're lying on the mattress in Ivar's room. It is our last night. Yesterday evening. I think of his hands, reaching out, touching me, oh, I miss those hands, Ivar. I love your penis, your soft, firm scrotum. He wanted to take me from behind, and I knelt on all fours, and it had been wonderful, we'd laughed, it was so good. Afterwards, I'd closed my eyes, lay on my back, listened to Ivar breathing. That was when I saw the skinny man. He was standing in the doorway. He'd taken off his clothes. The girl was lying on the bed, rigid. I tried to blot the image out, but it forced itself in on me. If you want the one thing, Johanne, you'll have to take the other. His long hair hung loose over his shoulders, slowly he turned. And then I saw. It wasn't a man; it was a woman. The bony hips, the slack belly, the flat breasts. She advanced towards the girl. I could see her huge labia dangling in among the crinkly hair. The girl wanted to turn, to escape from the bed, but she couldn't move. The woman walked over, she took her hand and rubbed it against her genitals, between the wet lips. The girl lay there with the small of her back pressed against the mattress. The odour of discharge. Slime. The girl's eyes grew bigger, as the woman put one of her breasts in her mouth. Then, placing a knee on the bed, she swung herself up and, kneeling over the girl, she lowered her sex and rubbed it into her face. Lick me, she said.

I sing, as though my song could erase these thoughts. But they keep coming. I pray to God for strength, for greater faith, for humility. This fog in my head, this exhaustion, this powerlessness, these endless images. I look at my feet. Are they a part of me? Where do I begin and where do I end? These hands, are they mine? These words? These thoughts? My own voice seems so far away, coming towards me from another place: talking, laughing, inconsequential, superficial. The rain. I watch it falling on the other side of the window, observe the uneven patterns of the drops on the pane, the dense grey colour in the sky that casts such a wonderful light. A dark light that makes me think about God again. You see, Johanne, it's like a circle, everything is interconnected, an identical picture, everything comes back to God. I shan't be afraid. I am not alone. No, you are not, Johanne. You are never alone. And now it's coming again. It always does when I'm happy or feel comforted or whenever someone is kind to me. I look out of the window again. The rain is trickling down silently, evenly, like the tears that cover my face. Perhaps God is in the water, in the raindrops. I put my hand against the cold pane to be close to Him. To be as close as I can without imposing.

Karin had left several messages on the answering machine. Where are you, Johanne? I feel like I'm losing you. I listened to her voice on the tape, but it seemed so distant. I didn't know what I should say. Then one day she came into the reading room, before ten o'clock. She knows I'm always there at that time, that it's my best study time. Johanne, she said, leaning towards me and giving me a cold hug of fresh outdoor air. I was glad to see her, felt my conscience prick, stroked her soft stubbly hair. Have you got five minutes? Never, I said, smiling and getting up. I followed her out onto the landing. I didn't want to go down to the cafeteria, it would take too long – besides, I'd have to buy something, spend money, and Ivar might spot me and come over, it would all be too much. What's going on? Karin asked. Why haven't I heard from you? Why don't you answer my calls? I love you. I care about you. I want to know what's happening. I'm going to America, I said. I must have looked idiotically happy. Karin just stared at me. Johanne, she said seriously, stop and think for a moment. Is it that boy in the canteen? Ivar, I said. He's a man. All right, she said, but how long have you known him? Always, I said. That's how it feels anyway. It's amazing. Just imagine, somebody loves me! Come on, said Karin. Now you're hurting me. You know I love you. And what about Unni? Have you thought about her, Johanne? Your sweet mother and all the things the two of you share? And what about God? Have you prayed to Him and asked for His guidance? She stroked my hair, brushing a few strands from my cheeks. Johanne, are you sure this is God's will? It's only six weeks in Pennsylvania, I said. I remember how proud I felt to be able to say it so lightly. To be young and impulsive at last. Karin shook her head. I feel like I'm losing you, Johanne, she said. There were tears in her eyes, she averted her gaze, looked down the staircase; someone was coming up, she turned her face to the ceiling, stood there blinking, the corners of her mouth trembling. We stood in silence before she finally looked at me. Then the tears flowed. You're growing so far away from me, she said, and from everything we share. She wiped her tears with the sleeve of the green woollen sweater she's so fond of. Johanne, she said, you didn't come to the Association meeting on Friday, and you weren't at the palace chapel on Sunday. It's an awful thing to say, but it even seems like you're drifting away from God. I had nothing to say. I didn't know where to start, she's left me with no opening, she viewed everything from a closed circle, with no gap for me to slip in. And my circle looked utterly different. I hadn't thought much about God recently, it was true. But I was so happy, and I gave him thanks whenever I remembered. It says somewhere that it's just as important to come to the Lord with our joy and I've tried to do that. I really didn't know how to talk to Karin. I felt drops of cold sweat running down my arms. Have you nothing to say? Karin asked. I just looked at her, as though I was waiting for an answer to come. I shook my head. I couldn't really say no even, because the truth was, I had a lot to say, it was just so difficult. We stood looking at each other in silence. I was struggling not to laugh, I can't take scenes like this seriously, they feel so pompous somehow. Karin began to walk down the stairs. Halfway down she turned and for a moment I was afraid she'd run back up and hit me, or hug me. But she walked on and disappeared. My head was bursting. I wondered if I should go down and talk to Ivar about what had happened. I decided to take a walk round the Social Sciences block to get some fresh air. Maybe that would relieve the pressure. I took the stairs, going in the same direction as Karin had a minute before, pushed the door open and went out. It's not true, I thought. Karin doesn't understand how things are. I thought I should feel grief at losing a friend, but I felt only relief. I felt free. What she'd said about God wasn't true. I looked at the withered leaves on the gravel and lawn, at the dark, wet tree trunks and the thin, spindly branches. A few leaves are still hanging on, I thought. We're holding out, clinging on in there. We are not alone. Despite everything, I felt a kind of painful joy. My confrontation with Karin had brought me some clarity and strengthened my relationship with God.

Ivar left the invitation open. He said he didn't know what it was with me, that he didn't quite understand, but he wouldn't push me. He'd be out there for six weeks to begin with, hardly an eternity, and my lectures would be finished in three weeks anyway. He wanted me to miss them. I'd take my books with me and he'd buy my ticket. We'd stay at a place in the country that some friends of his owned, an old house with an outside toilet. But it's warmer than it is here at this time of year, he said. He'd been before. There was a shower at one end of the house, also outside, and a veranda at the front where you could sit in the evenings and read. We might hear the grasshoppers still, and we'd watch the lights of cars in the distance, talk, play the harmonica and guitar, and listen to the radio. I saw the two of us being hacked to pieces by a gang of youths on the run. First they raped me, while Ivar watched on. Then they sliced off his extremities: his ears, nose, eyelids, lips. Blood and more blood. While I watched on. And then perhaps they let me live, and we both survived; Ivar permanently maimed, me torn, bruised. In the sticks, outside Pittsburgh, no car, the phone line cut. I thought of Mum. She'd be left alone here at home. And there'd be no way back once I'd left. She'd think I didn't love her. I didn't know how I could leave and still convince her that I loved her. I wished Ivar had never asked, that our relationship had been allowed to develop slowly. We could have let things happen at their own pace, without forcing things. I could live with Mum until I'd finished my studies, and sleep at Ivar's place now and then. Afterwards he could live with me at The Barns. We'd have a dog and go away on holiday.

Oh really, Johanne, he said. It was Tuesday afternoon. We were sitting with a couple of beers in the bar at Blindern. Ivar had bought them. I'm not keen on the taste, but Ivar reckoned it was something one should at least get used to. Yes really, I said. I smiled, I couldn't help myself when he looked at me like that, and his voice aroused me, I wanted to go to the toilets and have sex straight away, wanted to have him inside me, I couldn't understand why I'd waited so long, for something so delicious, and now I wanted it again and again. But I was tired too. We'd had some late nights, and I'd got up at the usual time, and my back was stiff. Yes, I repeated. He brushed some strands of hair from my lips, they were sticking everywhere, he leant across the table and kissed me. Two more days to go, he said. Stay with me tonight, Johanne. Do you want to? Yes, I said, I do. He gave me one of those fantastic smiles. But I *can't*. I could see my reply upset him. Everything made perfect sense in my head, but it sounded weird when I tried to explain. It looked obvious from the inside, but from the outside it seemed like a hollow excuse. I have to stick to my plan, I said. I can't go changing my habits, can't start spending nights away from home, it's important for my exams that I live a regular life, I said. But in the summer I'll be able to sleep with you all the time. Johanne, he said. His voice was so deep. My body said yes. I rang SAS today. There are plenty of seats left. We won't talk about it any more now, but I just want to say that the plane takes off on Thursday morning at eleven forty. He spoke slowly, so I'd remember what he was saying. I'll take the 8.54 Airport Express from the National Theatre. I'll wait in the coffee shop by the grey sculpture that's straight in front of you as you enter the departure hall. I'll wait there until the last call. The offer's open, he said. Then he said quietly, Everything in me wants you to come. He inclined his head and smiled, as though it was all so simple, not the least bit difficult, just wonderful and exciting. Everything in me. How could he say that so lightly? Why did he have to be so unreasonable? It was perfectly good here at home. America was just a fixation. And you can't miss three weeks of lectures; not when you want to go straight on to the professional programme. I felt my body ripping apart, my back about to shatter. I got up, saying I had to go to the toilet. There were students everywhere, pretty girls, couldn't he just take someone else with him and leave me alone? I went into a cubicle and sat down and it was as if my body emptied itself. It had been like that for days. As I washed my hands, I looked in the mirror. Eyes wet with tears behind my glasses. I wished I could split my body in two, give one part to Mum and the other to Ivar. Then they could both have their share, and I could keep my ribcage as a little raft on which I'd curl up and float away.

When I got home late last night the tins of paint were standing in the hallway, along with a big roller and blue tray, some white spirit and a little brush. I'd forgotten completely. Several days had passed since Mum was meant to buy the paint. I wouldn't get the decorating done before I left. Nor did I want to think about coming back, right now. It would have to wait. I tried to switch my thoughts off. It'll be all right, Johanne, everything will be just fine, I said to myself. I took the black travel bag down from the top of my wardrobe and started to pack. Ivar had brought me home. We'd been for a long walk, taking little detours, stopping to look at views, corners and road signs, we'd kissed, stood in silence under an extraordinary tree, looked at an old table in an overgrown garden. We'd talked and laughed. There'd been so much to discuss. In the beginning I'd wondered what I'd say when we were together, plan topics of conversation, try to think of things that might interest him. Last night we simply talked. So many new ideas came to me when I was with Ivar, thoughts I didn't know I had. It was as though we were walking together along an old familiar street that suddenly opened out and lit up, enticing, wondrous. Never-ending. I hadn't wanted to let Ivar go. But I had to, of course, since I was going home to pack. I'd made up my mind. But I still didn't tell him. I was looking forward to turning up on the train and making him happy. He was going to lift me up and we'd spin around and around. It had come clear to me as we walked. I knew that I had to go. I couldn't let Ivar slip away. He mustn't leave without me. The suitcase, my clothes, the walls, the floor, everything had clean, crisp edges. All my movements were precise. This was for real. I wanted to pack swiftly and be done with it, as if there was a clock hidden somewhere, ticking towards catastrophe, but so long as I finished my packing all would be well. I decided I'd send up a prayer before going to bed, and I had to remember to pack my Bible. I tried to speed up, but my body went so slowly, hanging back, as though it knew all this would come to nothing. But the decision had been made, I packed, my desire was so strong, as though my will could govern everything, triumph all on its own.

Johanne, yelled Mum from her bed. I'd been sure she was in a deep sleep. And I'd tried to be quiet. Yes, Mum, I shouted back. What? She didn't answer. She could just come here and see. Come here and see me packing. At the back of my wardrobe I found a chunky brown sweater that I'd knitted years ago and forgotten. It was soft and warm, and I wanted to take it to use when we sat outside in the evening; I'd put it over my knees and sit listening to Ivar's gentle voice as he experimented with ways of phrasing a new melody. We'd dream and make plans. Our hands would grow wrinkled together, old and wrinkled and happy. Johanne, said Mum. She was wearing her dressing gown and had a cigarette in one hand. What are you doing? Packing, I said. What? I'm packing. I'm travelling tomorrow, remember? I couldn't bear to look her in the eye. I checked what I'd put in the case, but I wasn't concentrating. I registered Mum lighting her cigarette and exhaling, then taking several drags, deep into her belly. I didn't think it would actually come to anything, she said. You didn't mention the trip again. No, I said. She was right. I'm not sure why I hadn't talked about it. I'd thought about it all the time. The trip to America with Ivar. It had certainly been going round in my head constantly; whether or not to go, if I could or should, if it was responsible. I'll be honest with you, she said, I'll be completely straight with you. Yes, I said. I feel cheated, she said. I didn't say anything. I thought we'd agreed that you were going to decorate the lounge? Yes, I said. And now here you are creeping about, packing in the middle of the night to go away. Just leaving everything behind. Yes, I said. There was silence. If she'd got the paint sooner I'd have managed to do the decorating. I'd asked her to buy it, but I hadn't wanted to nag, she hadn't seemed particularly keen. True, I'd promised to do it. True, I hadn't kept my word. And I hadn't told her anything. Mum went into the lounge and sat down, on the very edge of her chair. She stubbed her cigarette out in the ashtray, I heard it crunch under her finger. I started to cry. I'm sorry, Mum, I said. I'm really sorry I didn't talk to you, I should have spoken to you and prepared you, I know it's bad. Please don't be angry with me. Mum came and stood in the doorway, a hand resting on each side of the frame, the sleeves of her dressing gown draped like the wings of an angel. How can anyone ever trust you, Johanne, if you don't keep them informed? It's impossible to know where one stands, and you know my experiences with unpredictable behaviour, she said. It's not on, Johanne. You're a fully grown adult. Was she saying I was like that; out of control, without boundaries? That I trampled on people? That I was a psychopath? Suffering from an antisocial personality disorder, as it's called now. A condition characterized by a lack of empathy, an inability to imagine how others feel, or to put oneself in their shoes. To understand their pain. In a way that's true; I do find it hard to comprehend other people's suffering, how things feel for them, and I know I'm bad at offering comfort, I seem incapable of it. Maybe it's just the way I am, I thought, irrational and insensitive without knowing it. I'd been wrong not to talk to her about travelling. But I hadn't spoken to anyone, not even Ivar. I'd thought I was the only one who could grasp all the arguments, for and against, and that I was the one who ultimately had to decide. This was all my fault. Maybe she'd have understood me if I'd told her, she might even have helped me pack, bought me some pretty pairs of tights, slipped a treat in for Ivar and me to share.

Mum went behind the curtain and back to bed. Moments later I heard the reading lamp go off and saw the sliver of light on the lounge wall disappear. I finished my packing, toiletries included, but the will had gone. I watched my small hands moving among the folded clothes; perhaps I was hungry, low blood sugar. I sat in the kitchen and ate an orange, trying not to think whether the eating helped; I had decided to leave, those thoughts had no place. I washed my hands and dried them, put the clean clothes I'd wear tomorrow in a pile on top of my bag. I went into the bathroom and took a shower. I washed my hair to make it curl; it's lovely the next day when I go to bed with it wet. I brushed my teeth thoroughly. I wasn't the least bit tired, but my arms felt heavy. I put my red toothbrush back in the glass next to Mum's yellow one. Otherwise my shelf was empty.

I hear a key in the lock. Mum's back home. I've been waiting so long for that sound that when it finally comes it's too sudden and I'm alarmed. Just imagine if it isn't her. Or if she isn't alone. Perhaps Ivar's with her and they'll sleep together while I listen. Relax, Johanne. She's alone, I hear only her footsteps. Thin, hard soles against the floor in the hallway and then going through into the lounge, tip-tap, tip-tap. I bang on the door for her to let me out. Mum, I shout. You've got to come and help me. Mum! Hello, Mum! Hurry up! I hear her taking her outdoor shoes off. They must be wet from the rain. Maybe she's putting her others on, the ones that she wears indoors. I listen to her going into the bathroom. The door creaks. I can see her now, unzipping her trousers and sitting down. Why isn't she coming? She's in there smoking! That's what she's doing. She must be able to hear me. Or maybe she's got her Walkman on. I shout louder.

There's a knock on the door. I don't know how long I've been waiting since her return. Five minutes. Maybe ten. I'm sitting on the chair at my desk, looking out. The footsteps have stopped, perhaps she's walking about in her socks. Johanne, says Mum, through the door. Yes, I say. For a moment it's quiet, apart from the noise of the fridge humming behind her. The rain has stopped. The afternoon is drawing in now, it'll be dark soon, evening will turn to night, and then the day will begin again. I hear her sit on the chair, it creaks. She's in my seat, right outside my door. Johanne, she says again. I don't answer. When you were born and I held you in my arms... She stops. I say nothing. It's quiet for a moment. You are the wisest and loveliest person I know, she says. Which is why I gave you this day, she says. A sort of day of rest. To give you the chance to think things over. I don't know if I've done the right thing, but I pray that God will forgive me if I've done wrong. She waits. Anyway, it's done now, she says, and can't be undone. Silence again. I can hear her preparing her Winnertip machine and pulling the tape off her packet of tobacco. I wait for the sound of the flap sliding forwards and then back, the tap of the cigarette against the table, her thumb on the lighter as she lights up. I gaze out at the Virginia creeper. It is a dark red. My back feels supple now, nice and soft. The key turns in my door. The sound of metal rattles in my head as though the lock was inside me, then her face appears, she smiles hesitantly, exhales, extends the hand that's empty of a cigarette, bends down and brushes the top of my hair with a kiss. I observe her arm near my throat, the tiny mole on her elbow, the fine, downy hair, light brown. Are you angry with me? she asks. She looks at me with big blue eyes, leans in front me and lifts away my hair to see me properly. Her face is right over me. I feel her breath on my forehead and note the skin cream glistening on her neck. Answer me honestly, she says. The whites of her eyes are completely yellow, a blood vessel has burst, forming a delicate red web. I see the reflection of my own eyes in hers. And feel nothing.

Peirene

Contemporary European Literature. Thought provoking, well designed, short.

'Two-hour books to be devoured in a single sitting: literary cinema for those fatigued by film.' TLS

Online Bookshop

Subscriptions

Literary Salons

Reading Guides

Publisher's Blog

www.peirenepress.com

Follow us on twitter and Facebook @PeirenePress
Peirene Press is building a community of passionate readers.
We love to hear your comments and ideas.
Please email the publisher at: meike.ziervogel@peirenepress.com

Subscribe

Peirene Press publishes series of world-class contemporary novellas. An annual subscription consists of three books chosen from across the world connected by a single theme.

The books will be sent out in December (in time for Christmas), May and September. Any title in the series already in print when you order will be posted immediately.

The perfect way for book lovers to collect all the Peirene titles.

> 'A class act.' GUARDIAN

> 'An invaluable contribution to our cultural life.'
> ANDREW MOTION

£35   1 Year Subscription (3 books, free p&p)

£65   2 Year Subscription (6 books, free p&p)

£90   3 Year Subscription (9 books, free p&p)

Peirene Press, 17 Cheverton Road, London N19 3BB
T 020 7686 1941
E subscriptions@peirenepress.com

www.peirenepress.com/shop
with secure online ordering facility

Peirene's Series

FEMALE VOICE: INNER REALITIES

NO 1
Beside the Sea by Véronique Olmi
Translated from the French by Adriana Hunter
'It should be read.' GUARDIAN

NO 2
Stone in a Landslide by Maria Barbal
Translated from the Catalan by Laura McGloughlin and Paul Mitchell
'Understated power.' FINANCIAL TIMES

NO 3
Portrait of the Mother as a Young Woman
by Friedrich Christian Delius
Translated from the German by Jamie Bulloch
'A small masterpiece.' TLS

....

MALE DILEMMA: QUESTS FOR INTIMACY

NO 4
Next World Novella by Matthias Politycki
Translated from the German by Anthea Bell
'Inventive and deeply affecting.' INDEPENDENT

NO 5
Tomorrow Pamplona by Jan van Mersbergen
Translated from the Dutch by Laura Watkinson
'An impressive work.' DAILY MAIL

NO 6
Maybe This Time by Alois Hotschnig
Translated from the Austrian German by Tess Lewis
'Weird, creepy and ambiguous.' GUARDIAN

SMALL EPIC: UNRAVELLING SECRETS

NO 7
The Brothers by Asko Sahlberg
Translated from the Finnish by Emily Jeremiah and Fleur Jeremiah
'Intensely visual.' INDEPENDENT ON SUNDAY

NO 8
The Murder of Halland by Pia Juul
Translated from the Danish by Martin Aitken
'A brilliantly drawn character.' TLS

NO 9
Sea of Ink by Richard Weihe
Translated from the Swiss German by Jamie Bulloch
'Delicate and moving.' INDEPENDENT

....
TURNING POINT:
REVOLUTIONARY MOMENTS

NO 10
The Mussel Feast by Birgit Vanderbeke
Translated from the German by Jamie Bulloch
'An extraordinary book.' STANDPOINT

NO 11
Mr Darwin's Gardener by Kristina Carlson
Translated from the Finnish by Emily Jeremiah and Fleur Jeremiah
'Something miraculous.' GUARDIAN

NO 12
Chasing the King of Hearts by Hanna Krall
Translated from the Polish by Philip Boehm
'A remarkable find.' SUNDAY TIMES

NEW IN 2014
COMING-OF-AGE: TOWARDS IDENTITY

NO 13
The Dead Lake by Hamid Ismailov
Translated from the Russian by Andrew Bromfield
'Immense poetic power.' GUARDIAN

NO 14
The Blue Room by Hanne Ørstavik
Translated from the Norwegian by Deborah Dawkin
*'One of the most important writers in Nordic
contemporary literature.'* MORGENBLADET

NO 15
Under the Tripoli Sky by Kamal Ben Hameda
Translated from the French by Adriana Hunter
'Straight out of a Vittorio de Sica film.' CULTURES SUD

Peirene Press is proud to support the Maya Centre.

The Maya Centre

counselling for women

The Maya Centre provides free psychodynamic counselling and group psychotherapy for women on low incomes in London. The counselling is offered in many different languages, including Arabic, Turkish and Portuguese. The centre also undertakes educational work on women's mental health issues.

By buying this book you help the Maya Centre to continue their pioneering services.
Peirene Press will donate 50p from the sale of this book to the Maya Centre.

www.mayacentre.org.uk